S0-AYC-302

SHOOT THE PIPER

Also by Richard Hill:

Ghost Story

What Rough Beast?

Riding Solo with the Golden Horde

SHOOT
THE
PIPER

A
Randall Gatsby Sierra
Mystery

RICHARD HILL

Gloucester Library
P.O. Box 367
Gloucester, VA 23061

St. Martin's Press New York

94-1361 F Hil

SHOOT THE PIPER. Copyright © 1994 by Richard Hill. All rights reserved. Printed in the United States of America. No part of this book may be used or reproduced in any manner whatsoever without written permission except in the case of brief quotations embodied in critical articles or reviews. For information, address St. Martin's Press, 175 Fifth Avenue, New York, N.Y. 10010.

Design by Basha Zapatka

Library of Congress Cataloging-in-Publication Data

Hill, Richard, 1941 Oct. 15-
 Shoot the piper / Richard Hill.
     p.   cm.
   ISBN 0-312-10549-5
   1. Private investigators—Great Britain—Fiction. 2. Americans—Great Britain—Fiction. I. Title.
   PS3558.I443S56   1994
   813'.54—dc20   93-44046
                                                           CIP

First Edition: April 1994
10 9 8 7 6 5 4 3 2 1

To the memory of Gil Brewer, Jake Carnegie,
Jack Kerouac, and Mike Shaara—
all writers and teachers and friends,
all wild, all missed.

For Eady Payne Hill,
who made the first trip with me.

This is fiction. There is no "Green Man" pub such as I describe. Get busy.

Thanks to Hawthornden Castle, the U.S. panel for the Raymond Chandler Fulbright to Oxford Fellowship, and the copper and the SAS man in the pub near Durham.

And here's to you, Mrs Bottomley.

"It is important to have a secret, a premonition of things unknown. . . . A man who has never experienced that has missed something important. He must sense that he lives in a world that is in some respects mysterious; that things happen and can be experienced which remain inexplicable; that not everything that happens can be anticipated. The unexpected and the incredible belong in this world. Only then is life whole."

—Carl G. Jung

ONE

In World War I, German soldiers were instructed to aim first at the bagpiper who accompanied British troops—a strike against morale. Few pipers survived the war.

We had our own wars, including Vietnam and the war against the war in Vietnam, and the most conspicuous among us were often the first victims. And Jock MacLeod was always . . . well, loud, so when I heard his name on the phone again after all those years, I naturally assumed that somebody'd finally bagged the noisy, wheezy old bastard. And wouldn't that be rich? He'd been called the Pied Piper of the Apocalypse by *Rolling Stone*, a proto-Beat or Weatherman guru or post-modernist maximalist, depending on when you checked in on his raucous and inflammatory career. He'd built that career from fragments of other fragmented fiction-eers—a large portion of Kerouac, a dash of Mailer, some Henry Miller (his seductions, not self-destructions; Miller took care of himself) and some Kool-Aid from Kesey. Marinate in one of Hunter Thompson's killer cocktails with some sap from Robert Stone's Druidic *wird*, and, as old Bill Burroughs wrote, "garnish with nettles," and you'd be approaching the MacLeod Experience.

Lately he'd shown signs of having become a cranky and reactionary old lion of the nineties. Slowing down? Not likely. However he might lie and crow and dance and fuck all your women, you could not deny him his capacity for deadly and mind-altering substances. Even the drugs and booze he *hadn't* lied about would kill a dozen other men. Yeah, that was a habit he had, of partying with his friends until they died, then making a buck on their obits if they'd managed to become famous.

He hadn't killed Connie MacLeod, his faithful wife (and mother, he said), and it was Constance MacLeod, that Scrivener's Saint, who had me now on the phone from Florida. I hadn't even taken a case since moving west, so it figured that my first one would call me all the way back to the coast I'd come to dislike and back into a part of my life I didn't want to remember.

"You know he always loved you," Connie said. "Mr. Randall Gatsby Sierra, private detective."

"As I recall, he usually loved my girlfriends, too," I reminded her.

She sighed, a potent weapon. "He's lost. You're probably the only one who can find him."

I started to explain why I wouldn't do it, but she said, "There's money in it. Quite a lot, I'd think."

"I don't want your money, Connie."

"Not mine. A New York publisher."

I was suddenly interested against my will. "What's he done?"

* * *

It was brilliant, I had to admit. For years Jock had been promising a new novel to match his *Road Hog*, published in 1955. Apparently he'd come up with something called *The Pipes of Culloden* and been invited to New York to meet the season's editorial boy wonder, had taken the lad out for some old-fashioned MacLeodian decadence, then had—so to speak—snatched the ass right off him, disappearing with *both* a check he'd cashed before the editor had even considered getting up to face his hangover and the manuscript itself. Though Connie didn't mention it, there was probably a girl from Vassar involved as part of the prize. The editor was now short a girlfriend and a million bucks, and had no manuscript to show for it.

Just when you thought you'd banished any thought of Jock MacLeod from what remained of your adult, healthy mind, he popped up like a fun-house clown and made you smile and love him for a few seconds. Then you remembered what he'd done to you and cringed and tried to forget about him again. What about death? I wondered, Connie waiting for my answer. Would he cheat even death? Had he sold his soul for a devil's gift of a few more years of cultural plunder and would worry about how to dodge the bill when it came due, or was he Old Scratch himself?

I'd often thought of him along with Sir Thomas Malory, author of *Le Morte d'Arthur*. Malory wrote it only to pass the time in jail for having raped most of his and his neighbors' vassals' wives and daughters. Far from Robin Hood, he was a lord who stole from his poor peasants. He was charged with multiple murders. He made the Sheriff of Nottingham look like Mary Poppins. MacLeod had never spent a night behind bars, so he wouldn't have wasted valuable mischief time writing a book. Or had he?

"Is there a book?" I asked Connie.

"Yes. But I haven't read it. You know how he is."

"I do, so I recommend that we just write it off to experience and pray he never returns. Let the editor worry about it."

"But he's threatening to sue me, the literary estate."

The prick. If anybody deserved money from Mac-Leod, it was Connie. "Where'd he go?"

She sighed again. I sighed, knowing I was hooked. "He wanted to take a literary tour of Britain, to rediscover his roots. He's also been in quite a state about Scottish nationalism."

"Planning to be the new king, no doubt," I said, *"droit du seigneur* and all that."

Connie let it go. "Actually," she continued, "we know exactly where he was for more than a week. He wouldn't speak with the editor or me, but he was following the itinerary. Then he disappeared in Scotland. We think there might have been foul play."

"If he's involved, I think we can count on it. Probably trying to beat Malory's record and got himself ventilated by a pitchfork."

"There's no police record of violence," she told me. She really did seem worried. "Please, Randy, just call the editor. I told him you're the only one who knows Jock's mind well enough to find him."

"That's a scary thought. Then maybe I'll drop in on Dr. Hannibal Lecter for high tea. How do you find people who behave like fictional characters?"

"See," Connie said. "That's what I told them you could do."

I took the numbers and name and promised her only that I would call the editor. She thanked me and I sat on my island in Puget Sound, my head full of characters I hadn't met in years.

Jock MacLeod was the only man I've known who always had an edge on me, always some leverage, but after years I'd learned that his secret was simple: He would do anything to get his way—no, not violence but the bluster preceding it, after which he could fall to his knees, beg you for mercy, declare you to be his heart's only friend, and finish the evening with your wallet and your date. I was in grad school, an English major back when that could mean Korean vets, SDS bombers, and Hot Housewives Finding Themselves along with the usual complement of would-be bohemians, hopeless idealists destined for slavery in the public schools, and androgynous lit nerds. I'd already been trained as a Navy SEAL and busted up my knee in jump school, so I didn't have to go to Vietnam and kill people who read the same books I did. There I was, a shorthaired, shorter-tempered "trained killer" talking Byron and Shelley. I also worked undercover for the county sheriff to pay my way, but I was more a protector of than a threat to most of the people I knew.

We hung mainly at the Wild Boar: Bill Atwill, Don Coonley, Rob Hall, Ronnie Lowe, Eddie Perez, Michael Sullivan, Mike Wentworth, Non-Linear Lenny, and of course, Jock. Jock was the star. He played that bar the way the Phantom of the Opera played his organ, dancing up and down, reciting, singing, playing spoons on your head, sometimes just howling or grunting like a . . . wild boar.

Non-Linear Lenny cut him on crazy, though. He was a tenured art history professor whose superstition was that it was bad luck for any of his students ever to see him while he taught. He felt he was invisible to them at other times. He lectured behind a screen. Looking back, I believe he was adapting to schizophrenia as one could only in the universities of that period. He assigned grades based on his whimsical reaction to the flowers students brought in little paper cups they were to make to hold the blossom. And this was a state university, a new one north of Tampa that was supposed by everyone to be a straight-ahead commuter school, not some freak show like Columbia or Berkeley. But Jock MacLeod, with a little help from his friends, turned it into a Dionysian revel, a nursery for sedition, a training camp for cultural kamikazes. Jim Morrison was around for a while, very much under Jock's spell and drinking like his hero.

Not everybody could stand that much freedom, and not many of us remained serious official students. One of my best friends slipped me a note during a class on Milton's prose. It said: "Fuck this noise. I have a chance to be a Honda mechanic." He walked out and I never saw him again. I've often wished I'd followed. But hey, we had Ionesco and Dostoyevsky and Genet and Burroughs and, as he would always find some way of reminding us, the living presence of greatness in the form of Jock MacLeod. I swear he fucked every woman in that place who'd read anything beyond a textbook. It was hottest around 1967–70. The sheriff was pressuring me for some drug busts and asking about "anarchist" student groups, and I was trying to keep him calm. Once a month or so some crackers from the orange groves and swamps farther north would come down to "kick some hippie butt" and I would usually plant some drugs in their cars and drop a dime on them. It sounds treacherous, but it brought a fair number of them around—teaching them how it felt to be persecuted.

I called the editor collect at home. When I heard his sleepy voice I remembered that it was later on his coast and enjoyed waking him. "You called me collect," he said, as if I'd blown my nose on his tie.

"Seller's market, Mr. Ellis," I said. "You can hang up."

"No, wait. Mrs. MacLeod says you can find him. When can you come to New York?"

"Why do I have to come there?"

"To talk. About the job."

"This is the information age, pard," I said. "I don't like New York well enough to leave my little island here in Puget Sound and fly nine, ten hours just so I can see how big your desk is—unless you wire me the advance and we close the deal right here."

"Why are you so hostile?" he asked.

I wasn't sure myself. I'm not usually this much of a wiseass, smart-mouth P.I., but something about this editor and the age he represented . . . no, be honest. It was MacLeod. He'd branded me somewhere inside, an insult and injury but also a badge of a kind of honor you were ashamed to mention. Part of me wanted to believe in him again, save him, make peace. Part of me wanted to find him, tie an anchor to his ass, throw him into the North Sea, bring the money home to Connie, and never think of him again. Most of me didn't want this job. With this editor and Jock, there was no way it could come out right for me. I was afraid, and while some people get timid and depressed when they're fearful, I get aggressive.

But I couldn't tell the editor that, so I said, "It helps me catch the people I hunt. I don't like to leave my little island, so when I do, I go get the people and bring 'em in so I can come home and watch my favorite Mexican soap opera off my satellite dish."

"You own an island?" he asked, impressed.

"I rent part of it from a convent. It's just the sisters and me. They run the ferry dock and they have their own satellite uplink for their own programs. They call themselves the Order of Celestial Communication, but people call them the Satellite Sisters. I pay rent and provide a certain amount of security in case the Lord's caught napping."

"Nuns," he said, probably pinching himself, turning on lights. "What do you do for fun?"

"Hey, they're big fun. Best game players I ever ran into—Charades, Trivial Pursuit, Scruples. You'd be surprised. 'Course I only live here the summer months. Winters I spend on another island in the Sea of Cortez that I share with a whorehouse, the Sisters of Mercy. They're fun, too. Very classy. None of your border-town trash. They have an uplink, too, triple X, somewhat controversial, I'm told, in Utah and Alabama. I've had to bounce a couple of their customers, rich little snots from the states with snoots full of powder. But mainly it's a nice place."

"You're putting me on. Don't you get confused about how to treat them from season to season?"

"Nope. I found it works best to treat 'em exactly the

same. So that's my life. Now if you want me to leave it, you buy me two nights at the Carlyle, Tower Suite 3107, southwest corner of the thirtieth floor—they remember me—and a first-class ticket. I want a limo at the airport, and, if I take the job, we'll do the rest of the travel arrangements there. My rate's five hundred a day plus expenses." I was thinking about Bobby Short at the lounge piano and running downtown to catch Blossom Dearie at the Ballroom.

"What? Jesus, that suite's probably over a grand a night. Who makes that kind of money for—"

"You do, I'd bet, for letting an old con artist run a game on you. Actually, it's twelve hundred a night."

"I don't think I like you," he said. "In fact—"

"Good night," I said. "You can go find him yourself."

"Wait. All right. Tell me again what to do."

"Wire me a grand to the Sisters of Celestial Communication, Russian Island, Washington. It'll go to Seattle and they'll call me. That will be my advance. Buy the tickets, hire the limo, make the hotel reservations—I'm sensitive to noise and I believe those to be the most quiet lodgings in Manhattan—and we'll talk when I get there. If we agree, you give me a two-week advance and I keep track of everything on my plastic for reimbursement of expenses. If I find him right away you get money back. In fact, I'll make some calls from here, to the police, the Salvation Army. Maybe we can solve it without all the fuss."

"Salvation Army?" he said.

"They play a large role in missing-persons work in Britain. Police usually leave it to them unless there's a crime involved. I've been over there on a case. While it

◆◆ 9

did involve what was a crime here, it would have taken too long to do it legally, so I got the goods—the little girl—and brought her home."

"Who kidnapped her?"

"Her father was a British citizen of East Indian origins, and he thought he had the right to take the child and tell his American wife to go set herself on fire. He learned otherwise."

He paused for a while. "Thank you," he said. "I mean that's . . . reassuring."

"Well, we do have one thing in common," I said. "I know Jock MacLeod's a con man. Difference is, he can't con me. There was a time he could, and did. So I'm what you call motivated. What's all this roots tour stuff, by the way?"

"I got it all from the wife. Something about Scottish and Catholic heritage and the British literary tradition. But carrying all that cash and the manuscript and his . . . flamboyant style. I mean it's dangerous."

"I agree. So I'll try to keep him from stinging any more people."

He laughed dryly. "I meant to him."

"God takes care of drunks and loonies, and he's both," I said. "But he does need to call home. How'd he get that manuscript away from you?"

He groaned. "I don't know. For all I know, he drugged me. I was somewhat . . . impressed, and he—"

"You were used to people being impressed with you," I said. "Jock's immune to that. And you bet he drugged you. What the hell made you buy that book?"

"Have you read it?"

"I don't think so. Have you?"

"Of course . . . I mean, yes, I read it after a fashion,

I mean skimming—it is, after all, an enormous book."

"So's the Manhattan phone directory. Jock may have sold that to you for all you know. That's what you get for buying names and not books. I'll get as much of your money back as I can, and I won't tell anybody you got the Big Mac treatment, but I can't promise that pirate has a book worth recovering. He passed into fiction long ago. I think he feels it's other people's job to do the hard stuff, like writing. Oh, and I get a ten grand bonus if I recover both the manuscript and 90 per cent of the money. I'll draw up a contract and you'll get a daily log of my activities."

"Why not write it in narrative?" he asked. "You never can tell. Might be a book."

"I don't know if that makes you smart or double dumb," I said. "Do I get a million-dollar advance?"

"Your attitude," he said. "Have you by chance ever sent me a book? I mean, do you write?"

"None of your business," I told him. I gave him the addresses and numbers he needed and hung up.

Two

THE SISTERS SAID they'd take messages for me as usual. Their program covered much of the earth. Once I was working in Colombia and asked a rich client if he'd tune them in on his satellite dish. They'd put a crawler on the screen that read: GAT, CONTACT YOUR HIGHER POWER.

I called them from elsewhere and they gave me some information I'd requested from another kind of detective—a black hacker friend named Julius—and I learned I was being set up. I took my client to the bank and made him pay me all outstanding charges, then turned him over to the police for insurance fraud on a shipment of coffee he'd sold, then declared stolen, then hired me to find. Maybe he got my name out of a Stupid Dick Directory. I shouldn't be listed there.

I needed to make some calls, to the Salvation Army London headquarters, to New Scotland Yard, and to the last place Jock had been seen: the Lewiston Arms in Drumnadrochit, Scotland, on the south bank of Loch Ness. The time difference was nine hours, so I stayed up late playing Monopoly with some of the sisters, and ran Hayduke, my timber shepherd, around the island. Hayduke's the product of several crossbreedings of gray wolves with German shepherds so as to capture the best qualities of each. The wolf blood gives him longer legs, freedom from some inbred shepherd traits like hip dysplasia, and something of the wolf facial markings that my old husky, Jack, had—superimposed on the black and tan shepherd face.

It's a face that's hard to describe, but I love it. It's like a double exposure, with the gray and silver lupine mask dissolving to and from the black shepherd one, wild to tame. I paid a lot for him, and a lot more for his training, but he's worth it, and he keeps the women safe when I'm working where I can't take him. There's a thought: Ship him to Britain, give him a whiff of one of Jock's old socks, and hold tight to the leash. But MacLeod would find some way to ruin my dog.

I called so as to reach them on the morning of the next day. The lady at the Lewiston Arms said Jock had been manic and perhaps frightened. He had asked about Findhorn, a commune of long standing, and had even placed a call to there, but nobody recognized his name, so he'd called them, as best she could remember, giggling, "a herd of bog-trotting Druid pretenders living on sheep-patty mushrooms." The lady laughed all the way from Scotland. "The dining room was full," she said. "We all heard it."

"As Raymond Chandler put it," I told her. "Jock's about as inconspicuous as a tarantula on an angel food cake." She laughed some more and told me that he'd also called the islands of Skye and Lewis, and Harris, looking for relatives or something. She even had the numbers handy on her phone bill, and I wrote them down. "Any idea what he was afraid of?" I asked.

"I don't know. He asked if there were any priestholes in buildings nearby, or caves, and if we owned a shotgun or pistol. We didn't, but he was much calmer the next day. Actually, it was Mr. Benedict that calmed him down. They seemed acquainted." Our connection was broken. I called back to ask if she knew anything about Mr. Benedict.

"Quiet man, medium everything, just another guest. I don't know where or even that they'd met before. It just felt that way."

I thanked her and called the Skye number. I asked the man who answered if he'd seen anyone named MacLeod. Maybe I really could clear this up without flying halfway round the world.

"I'd say two dozen today," he said, "includin' me own face in the mirror. MacLeods, that is."

"Who are you?" I asked.

"Constable Bruce MacLeod. And who might you be?"

"I'm an American detective looking for another American named Jock MacLeod."

"Sure," said Constable MacLeod. "He called, told me he was a famous writer whose ancestors came from here. When I didn't offer a parade with bagpipes and the keys to the castle, he got a bit sour. Dougal, my counterpart on Lewis, had the same experience, so I'll save you a call there. I cover Skye and Harris. Maybe someday we'll meet his august person."

He paused for us to laugh.

"What is it," he asked, "that brings all the lost Scots around to claim their heritage, demandin' the clan tartan. My God, most of their ancestors were sold as near

slaves by the great chiefs they're lookin' for as ancestors."

"He's lost," I said. "I'm hired to find him."

"Well, I know the job must be taken seriously, but
maybe this fellow needs to be lost for a bit, if you
follow."

"That's me," I said, "the follower. If he shows, please
call this number." I gave him the convent's.

"I'll do that," he said. "And good luck to you. At
least your man isn't bashful. Should be a large target.
Well, I didn't mean it that way."

"But you're right," I said. "And that's what worries
me."

THREE
◆◆◆◆

THE CARLYLE WAS everything I'd hoped, as were Bobby Short and Blossom Dearie. The editor, unfortunately, was everything I'd expected. He wore strange clothes, like a kid dressing up in his gramp's 1940s or '50s wardrobe. He looked like a young, blond, good-looking rich kid who got a very expensive haircut every other day, trying to keep current. He had a corner office with two stunning views and a kind of constellation map with his authors on it as stars. He tried to look hard, and my guess was it worked most of the time—a guy who knows what he wants, a leader. What he wanted was to act like a big shot, and people were letting him get away with it because they assumed that in a world of kids, only kids could understand what they'd buy. If they took it away from him, my guess was that he'd throw himself onto the dark maroon carpet and have a tantrum, beating on it with his fists and feet and slobbering into the deep pile. Come to think of it, if I didn't bring something back pretty soon, I could see him with that deep pile in either fist as the security guards tried to yank him loose.

But I'd had my fun with him already, so we just

signed a contract and I told him of the phone calls. We hardly spoke because he didn't have a style to deal with me. Then I went back to the Carlyle to pack for a night flight that would bring me into London's Gatwick around 8:00 their time the next morning.

The plane turned back after an hour because the automatic cabin pressure device was not working, and it took a while to fix, and they had to test it before we could come back on board. I got acquainted with a beautiful black Dutch girl, a translator/actress, too young for me. Her name was Genevieve and her skin was the color of raw honey. We counted our blessings in being the only passengers with empty seats beside us. "Come visit if you like," she said as we reboarded.

Our next attempt to cross the Atlantic was briefly troubled by an attempted skyjacking.

I'd seen the guy when we were storing baggage overhead. He must have been a late arrival who'd missed the first flight but stayed for another and got lucky when we turned back. He put his soft bag under his seat. I smelled it, felt it—instincts developed over time. I felt the hair rise on the back of my neck. He was sweating too much and looked like a combination of a junkie in withdrawal and a speed freak full of meth. He was a Mediterranean type. I couldn't narrow it further because he hadn't spoken yet.

When the stewardess asked him to buckle his belt, he did so silently, frowning and closing his eyes as if to pull himself together. His clothes looked like something you'd buy on the lam from the first store you found, and his socks didn't match. Travelers tend to look better organized, and, while we all have good reasons to be nervous and uncomfortable when we fly, most of us

◆◆ 17

don't fog our own glasses when the cabin air finally begins to work.

But what could he have gotten past security? He sat on the aisle across from me. He'd made eye contact once in a kind of general sweep, and he seemed to register a possible threat from my direction. I'd been weighing the option of leaving my seat to tell a stew or asking her to stop and whispering, but now he knew that I knew he was Wrong. I decided against that. I'd try to take him on my own.

After we were airborne but before the seat-belt lights were off, he got up and carried a small bag forward toward the stewards area that separated us from first class, and I got up to follow him. He'd already unzipped the bag, so when he turned, his weapon was free and pointed at my belly. I had already fucked up by not jumping the guy before he cleared his seat, but for all I knew his sweaty finger was already on the trigger or detonator inside the bag, and he could have started the killing then and there. I'd studied ways to close on weapons, fakes followed by a quick shuffle in to get one hand on the cylinder, slide, or hammer while the other raised the barrel. With the lead grip, you yank down and back, hurting the trigger hand, then reverse, using the weapon to smash the shooter in the face with his own weapon. That technique assumed that the stray shot upward did little harm, but we were hurtling through air at maybe 25,000 feet in a pressurized cabin, so I waited. I tried not to think negatively. At least he'd kill me first so I'd avoid the shame of getting the other passengers killed. Empty mind, empty mind, breathe in, breathe out.

What we'd learned and practiced in SEAL training

was so thoroughly a part of us that once we decided which switch to throw, it was what we called "going on automatic." But I didn't have to throw any of my switches because I recognized the weapon pointed at me for what it was. Expressed in millimeter, he was packing something on the small side of the decimal point—.09 millimeter, maybe—and in caliber it would need some zeros after the point. We're talking about a barrel size of maybe .022 caliber, a barrel measured best with a micrometer. We're talking about a squirt-gun replica. I'd used one like it to train cats not to make a litter box under my porch and Scott Glenn, the actor, sells them in gun mag ads.

But it was a very good knockoff of the Ingram Mac II, so when he yelled, "Everybody freeze!" everybody froze except him—he was moving backward, Ingram aimed at me, toward the pilot's cabin—and Genevieve, who had a real umbrella, which she used to hook his ankle and trip him backwards. He was on his back, but he still had the gun pointed at me. "Why didn't you seize him?" Genevieve asked quaintly.

"Because," I said, "I want him to shoot me." I walked toward him and watched his desperate face and saw him squeeze the trigger. He had actually *loaded* it. It had batteries and a magazine of what I hoped was water, I hoped, and the stream hit me right where he'd aimed it. He began to sob as I took the gun away from him.

I had to protect him from several angry passengers, including Genevieve, who wanted to stomp him for frightening them so. His request was simple: "Please let me go to the bathroom before you tie me."

I kept the door open and watched him urinate while

everybody buzzed. I thought he might have a syringe or suicide pill. He just wanted to pee. Maybe the relief of this capture was just what he'd wanted.

The pilot decided to deliver him in Britain, which turned out to be his home, so we used the cuffs the copilot had in his locker and began to wrap him in duct tape to a forward seat. First-class passengers objected, so we moved him back to the smoking section, which he seemed to appreciate. I walked the aisles asking for tranquilizers and soon had enough. I guess they thought they were for me. I gave them to him with a bottle of apple juice and told him to relax. He was a very unhappy man and he'd be looking at a lot more grief come morning. Maybe we could all get some rest.

But Genevieve and I weren't sleepy anymore. She came back to my empty seat and we pretended to sleep under the blanket. It was really thanks to the poor nameless man taped to his seat in the smoke at the rear. But it was too cramped. In the grand old days of the DC-10s you could have intercourse undetected in adjoining seats; now there was barely room for your legs where your legs were supposed to be. So I went to one of the toilets aft and she counted to fifteen, then joined me. If anybody noticed, they wouldn't complain. We could probably have made love openly in our seats, having saved the plane and all aboard from what might well have been more than a wet shirt, but we joined the Mile High Club (safely) in the traditional location, the lavatory. Later we did sleep, cuddled together in my two seats under the blanket. I promised I would come to Holland soon and maybe even figure out how Chet Baker died.

* * *

By the time our gang straggled out of that 767 at Gatwick it was noon and we felt like survivors. Genevieve gave me a kiss and the passengers gave us a round of applause, and while she made her Amsterdam connection I explained to waiting authorities what had happened and told them where they could reach me.

Then I cleared customs and found the poor guy from Smith Car Hire holding up a sign with my name on it. I had briefly been a hero but was now again a lonesome traveler. You remember the feeling. It's reassuring to see your name in a strange land, even if you've been too busy to have been thinking about your loved ones—in my case the nuns, the whores, and a wolf-dog—and how sweet it would be to have a little yogurt and a hot shower and get into your own home bed.

But not yet, Mr. Hard-boiled American Shamus. First you must spend what seems the equivalent of ten bucks on a croissant, a Danish, and coffee at an airport shop, then get into your rented Fiat Panda compact, eyes squinted in the bright British sun that once never set on its empire, drive to a hotel somewhere nearby because your eyes are falling shut, and use your new kind of money or your plastic to get a room.

Drive? Shifting with the left hand, steering from the right side of the tiny and easily crushed car, on the left, which is to say the wrong, side of the road. I'd done it before. Driving is driving. No. Driving the British way is like driving the American way if, on your American drive, you're also trying to shave with a straight razor while looking in the rearview mirror. That comes close to describing the panic, the disorientation, the helplessness that made me want to shout, "Have mercy! I'm American. I'm not used to this." Angry people passed me on the right as I drove in what logically would be the slow lane—the shoulder or curbside one—which was their fast lane. They didn't blow their horns and curse and shake their fists in '86 when I was there on the Patel case, but they needed tourists then and our dollar was worth something. Now, as I'd already discovered buying my atlas in the airport, a pound bought what a dollar would in the states, only it cost two dollars to buy a pound.

It was, I realized, no less crazy to have the British driver on the side of the vehicle closest to oncoming traffic. We did the same in the U.S. I suppose the assumption is that you make better judgments when you're nearer the carnage of a head-on collision. But why have slow traffic on the outside and the autobahn imitators inside? Just to be absolutely contrary? Why not go all the way and make everybody drive backwards?

When the adrenaline dump of several near-head-on collisions failed to keep me awake, I knew I was in trouble, at the mercy, to quote that sad British song of the army *we defeated,* of "a world turned upside down." Welcome, Yank.

Somehow I got to Brighton. I used the Norfolk Resort Hotel because I was able to get into its entrance without setting off a barrage of horns. I didn't care if this was the one the IRA blew up—that was, I believe, the Grand—or if they planned to blow it up that night. I was tired. I didn't even ask my usual questions about the location of ice machines, elevators, or visiting Shriners, but accepted the only room they had. Why bitch? As one of Mr. Naipaul's characters said, "The world is what it is."

FOUR
◆◆◆◆

AND SLEEP, AS Shakespeare told us, "knits up the ravel'd sleave of care." The next morning I had the big English breakfast—perhaps the explanation for their empire or their soccer thugs: tea and coffee, of course, whole individual pots of either. The British tend to drink real coffee; Americans drink hot water faintly flavored with coffee residue. The English killer breakfast continues, first with cereals, cold or hot porridge; grapefruit and orange sections; yogurt; brown toast if so specified and marmalade. So far, so good. Could be righteous California. But then come two or three kinds of sausages, back bacon (cut like what we'd called Canadian bacon or ham), fried eggs or poached, fried mushrooms, fried tomatoes, two kinds of fried bread, baked beans, and the ultimate challenge (short of Scottish haggis), black pudding. It is beef blood with gobbets of fat, fried in a round patty, and it tastes like a tire fragment found beside the road, only slightly softer.

And then, restored, back on the road which had become my beat. In the states I worked the interstates, mainly looking for lost kids and people in a childlike state. I took a case only if it seemed it would bring good to someone good or bad to someone bad. Now I was still working the Road Beat, though these were British: The M's or Motorways were the equivalent of our Interstate System, and the A, B, etc., roads corresponded to our old U.S. Highways, State, County, and local roads. And my quarry was a man who defied moral judgment, unless he was making it.

Driving was a little easier the second day. I like Britain, especially England, even if it doesn't like me. I like their radio and TV, even most of the commercials; their clean and available public toilets; and their faucets that don't cut your hands but feel instead like a Bentley bumper. I like a country with towns and cities that give way directly—no sprawling commercial strips—to fields in patchwork-quilt patterns of white, mauve, blue clover; yellow rape blossoms; tan, cut hay; and grass green enough for Dylan Thomas. You've got to love a country that has Toad Crossings.

I drove to Rye, though it wasn't in the sequence of MacLeod's trip. I passed through Hastings, which looked a little more like Daytona Beach than when I'd last seen it. The Normans had defeated the Saxons here, and now commercialism seemed to have vanquished tradition. There were theme parks elsewhere on the southern, channel shore. I saw their brochures in petrol stations and thought it a shame. Everybody in Britain seemed to want to go to Florida, not satisfied to have brought Florida here. I thought I should warn them, but I'd written off my home state long ago. Besides, that many people wanting to leave the cool green summer of Britain for a sweltering, humid, billboard jungle in Florida bespoke hysteria on such a massive scale that the subject was probably dangerous to talk about.

I parked in Rye next to the King's Head Pub. I asked directions, then looked up a steep, cobblestoned Mermaid Street that led, the barman had told me, to the "author's house." The author was Henry James and his home, Lamb House, was just around the corner from the ivy-clad Mermaid Inn. There was no guest book at James's and the two ladies in charge seemed recent graduates of Dithering School, so I walked back down and stopped in at the small bar of the Mermaid. Barmen were my best sources, as long as I didn't drink their wares.

When this one heard Jock's name he reached up to take a photo from one of the uprights that framed the bar. The bartender had a head of curly brown hair, some of it falling onto his forehead like those photos of Dylan Thomas. His face was ruddy, but somehow his nose was pale, or remarkably paler. I'd never seen anything like it and could think of no explanation. "Is this the fellow?" It was. "Is he really important? I mean, I kept it just in case, but his name didn't ring no bells with me—not that I'm a heavy reader."

"Yes, he's important," I said, "but not as much as he thinks."

"He's written some strange stuff on the back." He handed the photo to me.

It read:

> Ex-patriarch Edward Abbey called expatriate Henry James "our finest foreign lady writer." Edward, God rest his desert soul, was our best redneck misogynist writer. I claim all the territory in between. Bold as Whitman to be great, "contain multitudes," and bolder to be a man.
> —Jock MacLeod

"What's to be made of the man?" the barman asked, his brow folded in earnest concentration.

"We may never know," I told him. "The thing is, he makes himself up. He's a work in progress, a talking book."

"Daft, if you ask me." The barman took a rag to the clean bar as if to wipe away the residue of MacLeod's anarchy and bombast.

"I know how you feel," I said, and paid him for my bottled water. I offered him back the photo and he seemed not to know what to do.

"I should give it to you," he said. "It means naught to me or my customers. They won't recognize him."

"Don't be so sure," I said. "I predict you'll get at least one a month who will, in season. It could even be worth money some day, or be important to a scholar."

"That's not it," he said. "It's like he's trusting me to do it, make it my responsibility, and I shouldn't let him down."

"That's how he works," I said. "Makes you part of the great story."

"Sounds devilish." He began rubbing vigorously again.

"And it is. I swore I'd never come looking for him, and here I am."

The barman gave a little shudder and tacked Jock's photo back where it had been. Somehow the wood around it was already faded, so it fitted perfectly into its rectangular space.

"Look at it this way," I told him. "It's a postcard. He wouldn't be on a postcard if he weren't famous, would he?"

His face lit up. "I didn't notice that," he said. "You're absolutely right."

I didn't mention that you could find that card only at City Lights Book Store, and most of them had been bought by Jock himself for just this purpose. He knew what he was doing.

I was almost out the door and worrying about the cobblestones and my bad knee when the barman yelled, "At least he's not one of that pop-star lot. They get those kids all stirred up—ravers they call themselves, used to be mods and rockers before that—all full of drugs and liquor, and they come down to nice seaside towns like this on bank holidays and tear it all up, including themselves. He wouldn't do that, would he?"

"He might be worse," I felt compelled to say. "He has been in the past." I hoped he wouldn't ask me MacLeod's views on the IRA; many on this south coast seemed braced for another bombing, like Californians for the Big One. He didn't speak, but he pinched his nose hard, as if to clarify things through pain. I understood why his nose was paler than his face. He was a man who didn't like complications and had developed that strange simplifying, probably unconscious habit. I'll bet MacLeod's photo is still hanging there.

Rye was a nice town, with canals and sailboats moored up among the buildings. I headed for Canterbury, finally a true pilgrim. What had Chaucer written of their motives? "The holy blissful martyr for to seke." Was that Thomas à Becket or Thomas More? I wasn't after a martyr. Perhaps the opposite, Yeats's "rough beast, its hour come round at last."

I'd finally relaxed enough with the driving to think freewheeling, the way I can do only while driving. I hadn't wanted to think about Jock again or any of the glory days that we'd thought we were living. Had we thought? Certainly we'd talked, riding Dexamyl or bennies, screw-top wine, sitting on steps as the sun came up, setting fire to palm fronds and dancing, climbing fences to swim in country club pools or jump naked into one of Florida's crystal springs with *botas* of cheap wine slung over our shoulders, under our women's breasts. Kissing Lauren at the Wild Boar bar until the shouting and assorted jungle sounds made us laugh. Going to Jock's trailer late one morning to see if I'd given him my wallet while he stood by and let me finish a fight he'd started, and finding Lauren there. The look she gave me and the drink he offered, as if nothing had happened. We were America's defense against the American Dream, and it was serious business, except it didn't seem so now. I'd call it child's play if it hadn't been so deadly. I didn't know how badly I wanted not to know what we had really done until this gig came along.

Our generation. Our degeneration. Now we'd reached the age at which one notices that maybe half of one's friends are dead. Fitzgerald had written in one of his notebooks that "It is in the thirties that we want friends. In the forties we know they won't save us any more than love did." I was thinking: And if they're mean enough to survive, they can come back to haunt us.

I was getting the blues, and I tried to shake it off. Surely there had been joy and freedom and sincere love more than we dared express today, and friendship. . . . Why was I driving this tiny Panda when Ellis was sending me first class? I would stop wherever I could and trade it for a Jag, with automatic. That would make me feel better. A CD player and some Handel and Joe Cocker. I downshifted into another goddamned roundabout and gave up the idea. I could chase Jock in a chauffeured limo and this would still be a desperado dust-bowl ride down a rutted road into memory's junkyard, complete with bad dogs. The bad Kerouac was even more depressing than the realization that it was as true as I could get it right now. I would have to face things I'd turned away from, make decisions I'd put off forever, answer questions I'd tried to believe no longer had meaning. All this from the hum of tires on macadam and the image—what must he look like now? I hadn't thought to ask the barman if Jock still matched that old photo—of Jock the Piper.

Wait, I had a recent photo in the file that Ellis had gotten from Connie. I slowed to pull over and somebody horned me. I slammed on the brakes and the same guy nearly rear-ended me. Yanking on the emergency break, I let the engine die, releasing the clutch with her still in gear, then jumped out and got a good kick into the left rear fender of the motherfucker. He thought about stopping, but people were blowing at him.

I was jumping up and down in rage, probably as much with Jock and myself and our lives as with this Brit, but I gave it to him, them: "Come on!" I said ridiculously. "I'll kick *all* your fucking limey asses. I'm an American!"

Nobody was taking. Back in the car, breathing heavily and red-faced and laughing, I looked at Jock's photo. The son of a bitch hardly looked a day older. He was looking straight at me, left hand raised as if to say, see, see what I can still do? And he was laughing. Whatever

Jock was, he hadn't changed, and I had. Maybe he was the personification of all that unfinished business, the tempter in my dreams, the joker, the pimp, dealer, the Pied Piper, the Big Liar. I had to do more than just find Jock. I had to figure what his power was and beat him.

FIVE

I'D SLEPT LATER than I'd planned at the Norfolk, and with the visit to Rye, I was late on the road to Canterbury. I noticed that English kids were still in uniform and still in school in June, when ours were tanning on beaches, consuming products, and flipping burgers to pay for it.

With very little warning I found myself in a large city at the evening rush hour. My fragile earlier confidence in my driving left me, like an actor "gone up" on his lines, and I found myself trapped in fast, frantic traffic heading I didn't know where. I felt like a cat tossed into a kennel of hounds. I looked for any way out. It came in the unlikely form of a car lot and later, after I'd stood outside the Panda, turning in confused circles, a car salesman.

"Where am I?" I asked him.

"Canterbury," he said, and we both laughed.

"Looks like New Jersey to me," I said.

"Look," he said, pointing, and I saw the cathedral rising beyond the wall on the far side of the snarling traffic.

"I'll never get over there," I said.

"Leave the car here," said my benefactor. "Cross up there with the light."

"You'll take my car in trade while I'm gone, and I'll come back and find . . . one of your—"

"We sell across the market," he said, still laughing, "but we won't make your Panda disappear." He pronounced it *pander*.

"My dad sold cars," I said. "I know."

"Only in America," he said, pronouncing it *Americur*. I remembered that the New England colonists had come from here, East Anglia.

"Just kidding. Thanks. Pointer's Hotel?"

"Here," he said, "I'll draw you a map."

I went to Pointer's first because the cathedral seemed overrun by modern pilgrims. The manager was a friendly guy named Bob. He had dark, thin hair, slicked back to suggest his skull. His eyes were sunken and his gaze direct and a bit too serious for a hotelier. His clothes hung on him in a way that suggested recent weight loss. He gave his own desk a wipe when I mentioned Jock's name—a universal reaction so far. "A man possessed," he said.

"How about I check in and then buy you a drink? If you have a room?"

"My pleasure," he said.

"I had a rough night last night. I'll pick quiet over luxury any time."

"I've got one in the back that I save for last, or for customers like you. It's nice as the others, but nobody nearby."

"You're a gentleman and a scholar," I told him, and it turned out to be true.

We went next door to the small hotel bar and had a Scotch and soda. He drank the Scotch; I drank the soda.

"I've heard," he said as we listened to the receding rush-hour traffic, "that he interrupted a lecture over there, and I think it was about the same matter, more or less, that he wrote in their guest book. He blamed Chaucer for retracting his *Canterbury Tales* because the church deemed them salacious. Here, it's in my book, too."

Bob left, and I helped myself to the soda bottle. He came back with his own guest book—not his official register—and opened it to show me. This was my second sample of Jock's handwriting, very different. It was nearly illegible, but what I made of it said:

> Chaucer confessed that in his life he'd written "many a song and many a leccherous lay; that Crist for his grete mercy foryeve me the synne." *I* would have said: "In which I hope Christ, in his humanity, may find a few laughs." Why revere Thomas à Becket for standing up to the king and then let the church bully one of our best writers?

"Do you know him?" Bob asked.

"From long ago. I'm hired to find him now. I don't think that he's what we'd call stable. Was he sober when he wrote this?"

"Yes. The only time I saw him that way. How did you know?"

"This is nearly illegible. The last I saw was a bold,

flowing cursive script. Means he was relaxed, which for him means loaded.''

"Ah, good, you *are* a detective. I'm very keen on Chandler. Wish he'd written more, but there's Ross Macdonald. What's MacLeod done?''

''Nothing, really. He just may not be safe in his condition.''

"Right,'' he said with that Monty Python ambiguity most Brits seem to use when they're buying time, not convinced. "He told me he was off for Rye, but you've already been there?''

"I'll go to his next destination. Did he seem worried?''

"Only about pub hours, which he found Victorian. Of course he's right. The queen rightly understood that if they were open straight through, little work would get done. She also refused to have her words broadcast on radio lest they should be listened to by men in pubs.''

We laughed. "Was he keeping company? Anybody seem particularly interested in him?''

"No,'' Bob said. "I wish I could help more.''

"You have helped. I appreciate your courtesy. I'll try to let you know how it turns out, since you're a fan.''

Bob hesitated. "I don't want to add anything to your already stressful day, but I won't be here long.''

"Better job, I hope.''

"Bit of prostate cancer, I'm afraid.''

I hesitated, not wanting to add the murder of my sympathy to his troubles. "Well, surgery,'' I said.

"A bit late, I'm told.'' I understood the directness of his gaze, the keenness of his interest, also his pallor and his no longer filling his clothes. "I'm fine about it. Shouldn't have mentioned it. Sorry.''

"I'm sorry," I said. "Why don't you get a second opinion?"

"Well, one automatically does those things."

"I'm a detective," I said. "Open up the odds. See three more surgeons at least. They're human."

"Well, false hope and all."

"Better than none," I said, knowing I was making it all worse, cringing at the stupidity of my remark.

"Maybe I will," he said.

"Humor me. I'll call you when I've found this bum and we'll have a big dinner on this pissant editor who's paying my bills."

He smiled, and it wasn't just to make me feel better.

I walked over to the cathedral, trying to shake Bob's death from my mind and take up the case. I couldn't, really. What was drunken Jock against Bob's diagnosis? But cathedrals are there for many reasons, one of them being to put things in a larger context. Normally they depress me because they're empty, except for tourists, but today it helped me, and it probably did Bob, too, daily, to . . . accept what was. Or maybe, like Becket, to fight it.

Bob had reminded me of Chandler. I'd last been in London on the Patel case and somehow hadn't gotten by to pay my respects at Dulwich, his public school in South London, or the Connaught Hotel, where he stayed often near the end of his life. Maybe this time.

With York, Canterbury was supreme among English cathedrals. The Church of England's two bishops occupied them, if only occasionally in the flesh. The pope had been evicted in spirit by Henry VIII, who had also ordered the shrine to Becket destroyed, fearing after centuries the power of another churchman like Thomas More who would stand up to kings.

It was to this southeast coast that the Romans came, and later their camp followers, the Saxons. MacLeod's itinerary listed Fishbourne, an excavated Roman city, next. It was one of the first, with Londinium yet to grow. Many of those early Britons had been Romanized as easily as their Anglo-Saxon conquerors of the fifth to seventh centuries were Christianized. But there remained the nostalgia for a nobler, native Britain personified by the mythical King Arthur and his perhaps prematurely Christian knights. Later, the Saxons embraced another mythic composite hero in Robin Hood, who frustrated the Normans who'd won the south country in a battle just down the road at Hastings, where I believe there are now Waterslide Worlds and miniature golf.

It seems the Britons were so called mistakenly after the mispronounced or misunderstood name of a king that the Romans, then in Gaul, thought to be the chieftain of this island across the channel. And while those in the south offered little resistance to the legions, the northerners gave them hell. The Romans called them Picts and Scots and built walls to keep them up there. The Picts, so called for their tattoos or "pictured" bodies, also had art that suggests to some scholars a Middle Eastern or Mediterranean origin. Some say Pictish was a language unrelated to all others and others say it was a form of Gaelic, but the profiles the Picts did of themselves (and elephants?) suggest a tribe that had come a long way.

Before them, and before the waves of Celts who

would become the Britons, Cornish, Welsh, Irish, and Scots, there were the fabled "beaker people" who built Stonehenge and Avebury, and before them the neo-lithic folks who buried their dead in long barrows, and before them the Old Stone Age cave dwellers or maybe other builders whose remains puzzle us still. The first Scots had wandered over from Ireland not long before the Romans came, and with the Picts became the "bar-barians" that the Romans could not handle. (It remains to be seen if Scotland can ever be completely pacified, with MacLeod's big mouth at large.)

I may not have all of this right—my reading on the plane was limited, though I did a lot of reading while on the Patel case—but my point is: Where does MacLeod or anyone else get off reclaiming a "native" Britain? York and much of the northeast lived for years under the Danelaw. Northern Scotland and the islands of Skye and Lewis with Harris were shaped by centuries of rapes and raids and actual occupation from the Vikings of what is now Norway.

If anybody has a beef here, it's the Picts, whose iden-tity seems to have been absorbed by the later Scots who, along with the Angles, at least had countries named for them—the Saxons already had Saxony on the continent.

The organization of Scottish clan tartans and such occurred in the nineteenth century, after most of Scot-tish history, in a time of Celtic nostalgia after the ban-ning of Scottish dress and bagpipes (as "dangerous weapons") by the English after the Battle of Culloden in 1746. It was Britain's second civil war and set in motion "The Clearances" of the Highlands, although there were other desperate migrations of Scots and Irish for economic and political reasons. Many of the Scots-Irish migrated to the United States to give sons to our own Civil War. They included my mother's kin. She was also half Huguenot French—Protestants, and guess from where. Bretagne or Brittany, the French Galicia, or home of the Gauls or Celts.

Centuries before, the beaker people seem to have migrated up from Spain, and much later many sailors of the defeated Armada swam ashore to become Irish. My dad was a Spanish-Cuban American whose ancestors were Gallegos, from the part of Spain called Galicia, after the Gauls or Celts. Gallegos, like French Bretons and other such people throughout Europe and even the Middle East (Turkey has its Galicia), favor bagpipes and fighting and poetry and song.

For centuries the English royal family have been a German dynasty. We are all mongrels, pilgrims.

What kind of pure Scots culture did MacLeod hope to find, or was he just playing our twentieth-century regression game in which everyone retreats to the smallest tribal identity possible in order to declare war on others, and we prove history has taught us nothing? Eastern Europe was turning into something like what Britain used to be; now, here was MacLeod, with his figurative bagpipe, to stir the dogs of war.

I went back to Pointer's and had another drink with Bob, and we talked about history. I remembered I hadn't eaten and neither had he. I asked him what he fancied most, no limit, and he said Szechuan—there was a little place a few blocks away. We decided that we'd prefer eating in our own bar and called to order something called Emperor's Glory "take-away," as they

say in Britain, and they got it over fast and hot and *hot*.
Bob used chopsticks and I used a fork—I use a fork to
cut bites out of spaghetti because that righteous use-a-
spoon-and-roll-it-up method leaves all the sauce on
your plate. In a normal meal I was sure Bob used his
fork left-handed, European, and I used my right. He
drank more Scotch and I drank more soda and tea. I
said *tomayto* and he said *tomahto*. Nearing the end of our
Emperor's Glory, I said, "Good or what?"

He said, "Bob's your uncle," which I thought was
Canadian. I told him about how I wanted to visit Chandler's places and he said he'd meant to do it, too. His
fortune cookie read: "You are about to embark on a
wonderful journey." Mine read: "The one you seek
may be yourself." We laughed. We said good night.
Tomorrow I needed to stop philosophizing and find
MacLeod before he started World War III.

Six

THE NEXT DAY I bought two of those phone cards from a news dealer. It's a good system, especially for somebody doing what I was. When your time card is used up, you buy another. The card-slotted phones are all over Britain.

But since I hadn't checked out of Pointer's yet, I used my room phone to call ahead about Jock. His itinerary put him at Brighton on the second night after his now-confirmed visit to Rye, but the Four Seasons said he'd never arrived, though they were charging him for not canceling in season. I called his next hotel at West Lulworth, and he'd been there, but not until his fourth night, so he'd found other lodgings. What he'd planned on the way was Jane Austen's house at Chawton, then Fishbourne, then the Castle Inn at West Lulworth. It hit me again what a deadly missile this old drunk was. Christ, *I* wasn't qualified to drive here and I'd quit drinking—for which Jock never forgave me. I felt more and more confident that what we'd eventually find would be his body in a rental car in a ravine in the northernmost moors.

Damn! What kind of detective was I? I called Smith's,

who'd rented to Jock as well as me, and they said the car had been returned on time in London, where it was picked up by one of their drivers and returned to their office in Rotherham. It was parked near the Alpha Royal Hotel as arranged, and the keys were at the desk, so nobody could describe who parked it. I called the desk and got a clerk who vaguely remembered a medium-size man with dark hair leaving keys for Smith. That wasn't Jock. I asked if anyone named Benedict had been around. No.

I called Fishbourne and cajoled the lady who answered into checking the guest book. Zip. So I said good-bye to Bob-my-uncle and headed up to Chawton. Bob and I hadn't talked about his death again, and we managed a friendly and unsentimental farewell. I said I'd call him and expected him to be there. No Benedict. Probably one of Jock's millions of drinking buddies for a night, Soulmates, Kindred spirits, willing to empty their wallets while Jock filled their heads with wonderful, mad noise.

The British have learned to live with narrow roads, like the rest of Europe. These are historic roads, some of them laid down upon not just Roman routes but Roman roadbeds. One of the ways the Brits have managed is to park their cars in front of their houses with their ass ends hanging out into those narrow roads. I wondered how I did it, deciding right-of-way with large lorries almost by instinct, but it was working better.

I wondered about boot fairs, their equivalent of our flea markets or garage sales; about what might be offered at the Philippine Craft Fair or the All-Kent Soul

Singing Competition. I listened to a French AM station with some really bad pop and BBC-2, with an anachronistic, friendly, Arthur Godfrey kind of chitchat and some of the strangest records, like Jeannie C. Riley's "Harper Valley P.T.A." I heard Gaelic on a weak station from Wales and knew I'd get it more clearly as I chased Jock out toward Cornwall and Wales. It sounded like a combination of Hebrew, Portuguese, and Scandinavian. I remembered that Portugal was named Port of the Gauls. I watched magpies and starlings.

It was early afternoon when I got to Jane Austen's home in Chawton. Like some other shrines, it was the main industry. When I asked about Jock, the woman on duty said, "Oh, you must speak with Mrs. Smythe-Chipping. She's quite worried about this." I walked around the tiny house as I waited, feeling like Gulliver in a Lilliputian home. What could account for such a sudden increase in the size of our race? Had the large ones been sent to the colonies in order to breed citizens more compatible with a small island and ancient homes?

Not likely. There were tall Britons then and now—Mary Queen of Scots and Graham Greene were over six feet—and they must have carried bumps similar to the ones I had now. Actually, my bumps—one just this last half hour in the Austen home—were merging into one large knot. By the time I left Britain it should have added another inch to my own height and taught me an embarrassing flinch when I walked through doorways.

Smythe-Chipping? What had kept certain names here in the sceptered isles while other weighed anchor for Australia, Canada, South Africa, the United States, and other colonies? Perhaps a censor unrecorded or later purged who said, "You Favershams, Smythes, Chippings, Hoggs, and Piggots, go home, and the same for you, Nigel, Cedric, Trevor, Colin, and hold there, Basil, Ian, Gareth . . . some confusion there? I see. It's Gareth who must stay. Garths may immigrate to the San Fernando Valley of California in 1980. Only Jewish Simons may board. Otherwise, all biblical names may immigrate. But no Liams, Alistairs, Alastairs, or any spelling variant, and no Emmas, but we'll do the women later. Anyone named Buddy, Bubba, Sonny, Junior, or Chip must leave on the first ship or face hanging. All right, move along smartly now."

I was standing in Miss Austen's bedroom doing this silly riff when Mrs. Smythe-Chipping arrived, clearing the door top by a good four inches. "Hello," I said. "I'm a friend of Mr. MacLeod."

"Thank you for waiting," she said. "I haven't been able to get that poor man out of my mind." A disease until recently confined to the New World, I thought.

"He was quite drunk," she said. "May I inquire if that's usual? Perhaps some recent grief?"

"It's quite usual, but he's an emotional man, a writer."

"So he said. I wish you could have seen him. He sat at Miss Austen's writing desk like a giant on doll furniture. I feared he'd break it. He told me that he'd written standing up atop refrigerators like your Thomas Wolfe, and seated on the edge of a bathtub with a commode top as his desk, and using a wire service roll of paper that fed continually through his typewriter, a scheme he credited to your Mr. Kerouac."

"I'm surprised he gave anyone any credit," I muttered, but she went on as if she hadn't heard me.

"Then he did the most extraordinary thing, and I haven't been able to get it out of my mind. He opened the armoire in which we keep Miss Austen's wedding dress, and he began to weep, great sobs after a while, trying to talk but not succeeding. Something about her dreams of happiness, marriage. It was altogether touching and troubling, and when Mrs. Worthington saw you, she knew I'd want to come. Will he be all right?"

Hooked another one, Jocko. But to her I said, "In my long experience with Mr. MacLeod, he's proven to be a survivor—resilient, emotional but resourceful, too. This is a difficult time in his life. Men experience . . . well, times of adjustment, self-judgment, doubt about what they've accomplished. I'll tell you the truth because it's important, and, if he sensed your concern, as I'm sure he did, he may try to contact you again. You must call this number." I gave her the sisters' number. "Don't tell him or he'll talk you out of it."

"What would happen to him?" It occurred to me that she was likely a widow, and the flush of her cheeks suggested a protective, caring, interested woman—exactly what Jock did not need.

I lied. "He won't admit it, but he's a diabetic. He needs to be in the United States with his doctor and . . . wife." I paused to let it sink in, and watched her color deepen and darken. "Drinking so heavily and neglecting his insulin—well, the results could be catastrophic.

"He began with the good idea of rediscovering his literary roots and celebrating the sale of his new book.

It got away from him. If he contacts you, call and I'll come help him."

She seemed firm in that resolve. "Is his early work available?"

"Yes. *Road Hog* has been a steady seller all these years. I'm sure you can get it. Perhaps not in the library."

Mrs. Smythe-Chipping was attractive in this light, radiating a kind of moral or . . . devotional beauty, the attractiveness of someone with what she had every reason to believe was a chaste passion, similar to Jane Austen's? Wait until she hit page 5, the Hell's Angels' gang bang at the Quaker retreat. Jock's book had been banned over twenty times in various locations by people who never got further than page 5. It would be interesting to see Mrs. Smythe-Chipping's color then.

"I'll get it," she said bravely, "and if I hear anything, I'll call."

SEVEN
◆◆◆◆

I CALLED AHEAD for a room at the Castle Inn in West Lulworth and hit the road—120 miles, as I reckoned. Hardly worth getting into the car, for us in the Road Hog Generation. The radio told me that Britain was having its regular summer trouble with "hippies" trying to use Stonehenge to celebrate the Summer Solstice. There was also a protest led by the rock group U2 on the beach near a nuclear reclamation plant at a place called Sellafield, on the Irish Sea, west of the Lake District. It was the only such plant in Britain, designed to break down nuclear waste and store it safely. Uh-huh.

I stopped into a pub and found myself sharing a table and the subject of hippies with the Entwhistle family of "traveling persons": Joe, his wife, Alice, and a shy boy of twelve or so named Teddy.

"Hippies are dirty people," Joe told me as we ate mixed grills, a combination of five fried meats that make up the British pub's most deadly food offering. Chops of beef, pork, lamb, and I'm not sure I want to remember the others. "They don't bathe," Joe continued. "They don't work, and they live in their filthy vans and buses. They're not the same as Gypsies, who've been with us a long time. Gypsies will steal, but they do at least have some order in their lives. Some do paving, and that's a crime, because it washes away with the first rain. I dislike it when the press call us hippies or Gypsies."

"We're hardworking people," Alice said. "Middle class." Teddy began to look down at his lap, but Joe took to the subject.

"We just had our vacation on the continent. I wouldn't recommend France for anything. And Monaco," he snorted. "I refused to even take a picture of the place. The food was a little better in Italy, but everything was so dirty there, and noisy. Switzerland, now that's the place to go. Better chocolate even than France, right, Teddy?"

Teddy nodded his head like a boy admitting a crime.

"Teddy gets his education as we travel about. He did right well last term in his maths."

"You travel for your work?" I asked.

"Right. Mainly I pave roads—that's like now in the summer when it's warm enough to work the asphalt. We park our mobile homes in a caravan with other traveling persons, which is what we are, not Gypsies or hippies. A few years back the hippies wanted to buy an old freighter at Portsmouth or somewhere and sail it to Holland, where they can get free drugs. They have their own social worker who follows them about so they can sign on the dole, and they were going to take him along, too. The government even approved it, but they couldn't raise the money or the gumption. There's a mess, I'll tell you. We should have passed the hat to get 'em out of the country. Now they're mucking about

Stonehenge again, useless buggers. Think they're part of some lost culture. I'd say they was lost. Ravers and blaggarts and bums half naked and high on drugs. Green hair, rings in their ears, noses, even their unmentionables. It's a disgrace.''

Teddy looked up, briefly curious about the unmentionables. I'd guess nipples, from my own experience with outlaw biker mamas and our own punks.

Joe became expansive as he filled with meat. "Get Mrs. Thatcher back, she'll put a stop to that. Some of the lads on me crew are muscle boys, body builders, skinheads, you might say, but clean. Big boots. Do a job on that mob, they would.''

I would have liked to stay and learn more from the Entwhistles, but I had a long way to drive. Before I left the pub, though, I followed an intuition and called the number Connie MacLeod had given me for Winston Oberon, son of Huxtable. Somewhat to my surprise, he answered. I told him my purpose.

"He was here, all right. I offered him a room, but he said he had a hotel reservation. Then, when I looked out the next morning, there he was, sleeping in his car. He'd rented a big Ford Granada, so I reckon he was comfortable enough.''

I liked hearing "reckon" again. "Drinking a lot?'' I asked.

"An understatement, even by our standards. I'm still recovering and have got a deadline, or I'd invite you for tea at least.''

"You're very generous to talk with me, and I do wish to convey my respect for your and your father's writing.''

"Wait a moment, you're Sierra,'' he said. I waited,

mind turning slowly, half pleased, half deeply suspicious. "You're the copper, his former student, the commando chap. He went on and on about you."

"I can't imagine him doing that. I mean, I haven't had any contact with him for years. We're not on the best of terms."

Mr. Oberon sounded excited by his unexpected role in all this. "He knew you'd be along after him, asked me to remember the name—Randall Gatsby Sierra's hard to forget—and when, not if, you came along the trail—these are his words—to tell you that the fox is the hound's best teacher. By God, this is fun. Come on by and I'll see if I've got another drunk in me."

"I quit, and based on what you told me, I can't afford the time. Another time I'd love it. God knows what he's up to. Did he let on at all? You must know he's in serious trouble, from his health to the possibility of his arrest for fraud and I don't know what else. Did you get any sense of his purpose here, especially now that it seems he meant to disappear? Also, did he mention a man named Benedict?"

"No. He called us both reluctant Tory converts, and I suppose there's something to that. We're both embarrassed by Reagan, Thatcher, Bush, Major, but we've also lost respect for the liberals and socialists. I must say, he didn't seem to have thought it all through. I don't find him a political creature, or really an analytical one. I think he's taken up Celtic separatism and Catholicism as more of a statement of dissatisfaction, alienation, than a solution. I understand your Jack Kerouac did something like that, and I never thought of Graham Greene as a potential anchorite, monk, even a regular churchgoer. Perhaps not coincidentally, Mac-

Leod planned to visit the Benedictine abbey at Down-side soon. Maybe that's your Benedict. He loved the name—a Beat name, he called it. Said he'd been on the phone a long time with one of the monks. He seemed relieved."

"Did he mention his next lodgings?"

"Castle? Is that it? On the south coast in a little place—"

"West Lulworth?"

"Exactly. This is fun. What's his game with you, do you know?"

"Haven't since the beginning, in the sixties, except that it's just part of his larger game with everyone. Maybe this time I can run the fox to ground and shake it out of him. May I leave you this number to call if you hear from him? Or if you think of anything else?"

I gave him the sisters' number and my own itinerary, thanked him, and said good-bye.

"Tallyho," he said. "I hope you'll write all this down so I can read it."

"Somebody should do some writing. We're far too busy acting. We've cut to the chase and I don't even know why."

"Surely MacLeod does," Oberon said.

"I'm not at all sure of that. He's run on instinct as long as I've known him. Thanks again."

"Good hunting."

I called the sisters, hoping for something. Nada. But there were whales in the sound and Hayduke seemed to be howling to them, and the sisters thought they were communicating and put the camera and mike on it and broadcast it to the world.

EIGHT
◆◆◆◆

I GOT SERIOUS about getting to West Lulworth, so of course I got seriously lost in a maze of motorway construction around Southampton. But it wasn't getting dark until around eleven, so with some generous directions (Brits outside their cars, like us, tend to be friendly), I found myself driving through land similar to the Oregon or California coast, with saltwater-wind-made bonsai evergreens through the beautiful New Forest, which was actually planted long ago, and winding down B roads to West Lulworth, a village of maybe two dozen homes, four inns, and a ramp to the sea that I found by getting lost. A sign pointed to a cliff walk to Durdle Door, a huge rock against which channel waves had been beating since long before Matthew Arnold heard in them the sound of receding faith.

The Castle Inn was a Tudor-style building that might actually have been built then. The roof was thatched, thatching still being a thriving trade in Britain. There was a patio in front with Cinzano umbrellas over the stone tables. I walked in exhausted and saw a woman who made me feel rested and alert, peaceful but excited. She was behind the desk, just around the corner from a moderately noisy bar. I rounded a corner to greet her on the back side of the desk and hit my head so hard on an ancient beam that I yelled, "Jesus!"

"Ouch," she said sympathetically. "That's the Jesus beam, all right. We padded it, but you're too tall. You walked under the padding and hit the higher part. I was just about to warn you."

"I won't *be* tall when I leave this lovely land of yours. I reckon I'll be about a five-foot-five-inch man with a permanent foot-long horn, the unicorn."

"Another damn poet," said somebody around the corner in the pub. "Yank, too. Watch out." It was friendly banter. I had a bad moment, nausea. Jock had been here, sprayed everything with his musk and left. Please, no.

"Let me see if you're bleeding," she said, but I wanted to look at her. She was all over a light honey color. Her hair was braided and hung to the middle of her shoulders, which were wide and well defined, and a lovely back open in a summer dress to where a panty line should be but instead were more light honey or dry sherry skin and the very finest fuzz. Yes, peach! It was honey and peaches and cream.

Her face was mainly open and lovely, everything in proportion, the whole better than the sum of its parts. It was late and some of her hair that had been pulled back to braid had escaped to make a kind of halo of fine curls around her face and ears. I figured my take on her eyes as slightly suspicious or guarded was explained by the circumstances.

"I want to look at you," I said, "not lean over and show my bleeding phrenological casualty of a cabeza," I said. From the pub I heard, "Woooooo."

"Sometimes we have to do what we're told before we get what we want," she said, and the pitch rose in the pub. "You lot shut up out there. Sing a song." Then, to me: "I'm Emma Poole."

"My name's Sierra." Now I saw that her eyes could say several things at once, but figured we all do that and so what if she's human.

"Leave your baggage and come outside. We need to talk. No, wait, I'll call Shirley. These lads'll be drinking and crowing late. You'll want a quiet sleep."

"Maybe he don't wanta sleep, Emma, love." A voice from the pub.

"I'm not your love, Jimmy. You'll find your love wrapped around that pint glass." Emma came out from behind the desk and suddenly we were standing close while the bar laughed with Jimmy, and when we bent over to grab my two sea bags it was all I could do not to touch her golden hair and touch her radiant face and kiss her, and we nearly did.

She stood first, blushing. "Like a drink to unwind? We can sit on the patio and get the main stuff said so you can rest and take up again tomorrow."

"Soda water. Two or three if all you've got is those little bar bottles, and a pint mug for it with lots of ice, please. I'll drag the bags."

"He said you didn't drink," Emma said, turning back to the bar. "Mind your head." Yes. Jock. *Droit du Seigneur* again?

I banished Jock from my thoughts, waited for my order, and walked behind her, enjoying her long legs and high rump, but most of all, the long, loose-hipped stride of a country girl, or, like the rich, horsey girls I'd seen at Sweet Briar, somebody pretending to be a country girl. For all the solid confidence of the walk, her calves were not thick but clean and well-shaped, and her ankles, too. I could walk a long time behind this woman, on dirt roads, footpaths, through deserts or swamps, to sod houses, caves, wigwams, yurts.

It was cool and pleasant outside, and still not fully dark. There was a table with three British bikers near us. Out beyond the stone wall were their bikes: a very recent Harley-Davidson Sportster—made in the U.S.A. with Japanese parts—a classic Norton Commando made here, and a vintage four-cylinder Honda 750.

A small car drove up with its radio blaring. A boy about nineteen got out and headed into the inn, probably to ask for directions, but he left his radio on.

"Mate!" said one of the bikers, loud enough for the kid to hear over the radio. "Would you might shutting that? We were having a conversation."

The kid went back and, to our amazement, turned it down very slightly. As he came back through the tables, a second biker said, "We don't want to hear it a little bit. We don't want to hear it at all."

The kid played his last card: "I thought this was a free country." American, of course. The bikers looked at each other as if to take that in.

The third one handled it. "It's not free if what you're doing is bullying others. You might try reading John Stuart Mill's essay 'On Liberty.' Meanwhile, turn it off or we'll put you in the boot and call your agency to collect the rental."

The kid jumped into the car and screeched away, radio still at volume. Number one biker said to the others, to the patio in general, "Some people are animals." We all laughed and applauded and the bikers bowed.

"How do you fellows feel about toad crossings?" I asked, a little giddy. Number two decided to field that one: "I try and avoid hitting any of the little creatures, but if it was me or him and I squished Mr. Toad, I wouldn't lose no sleep over it."

We heard the radio still, joined by a horn in the distance, a steady sound. "I know what he's done," Emma said. "He was in such a hurry that he missed the turn and drove straight down the ramp into the sea."

There was laughter and applause. "Shouldn't we go help him?" someone asked.

"The Lulworth Cove's right on the water," Emma said. "They're open tonight. It's their duty." Soon the horn stopped, then the radio.

It was a magic night. The weather had been sunny or partly cloudy since my arrival, hardly a drop of rain. It was near midnight and not yet completely dark, and I was in love. I drank my bottled water and looked at Emma. "We may not have much time," I said.

"A good portion of our population your age or older was fathered by Yanks with that same line," Emma said, smiling.

"Just think about it."

"I have been," she said.

"Now, Jock."

"First, if you've quenched your thirst, let's get you checked in at Shirley's while we still have some light, and I want to show you some things. I think Frances can handle the bar. I'll ask her. Then we'll drive down to Shirley's and walk down to the sea."

I left my bags where they were, and while she asked

Gloucester Library
P.O. Box 367
Gloucester, VA 23061

Frances, I called again for messages. Sister Sarah said Hayduke was still howling and she wanted to talk more, but I told her we'd catch up next time.

"So you're hot on the trail," she said. "The game's afoot. But is the jig up?"

"Not yet," I said, laughing. "I'll let you know."

"Sometimes it's better to keep the jig down," she said, "if you know what I mean."

"Sarah, you're psychic."

"I certainly seem to be. God's gift. No credit to me."

I promised to be careful and rang off. It sounded as if Frances wasn't happy about taking over the Inn alone.

We drove down to Shirley's Bed and Breakfast and I quickly checked in and dumped my baggage. Then we walked past the Lulworth Cove on our left right down the ramp to the water. The boy's car was gone, either towed away or taken out with the tide, which was in flood, lapping high onto the ramp. "The sea of faith was once too at the flood," I said, mangling Matthew Arnold.

"Ah, love, let us be true to one another!" Emma said. Then she surprised me. "Jock told me you could parachute into the sea, swim up underwater, and crawl ashore undetected to have a drink—of soda—at the pub and the favors of the best woman there, your origins unsuspected."

I didn't know whether I wanted to disagree with that or not. "Balderdash," I exclaimed. "MacLeodian hyperbole! It's MacLeod who can't be detected, by me, the detective."

"I'll tell you what I know," she said, but just then we heard a guitar, a tambourine, and a harmonica, and the pub nearby burst into song, Bob Dylan's "Like a Rolling Stone."

"They're doing it again," Emma said. "You should have heard it the night Jock got them going. Let's go up and sing."

Soon we were weaving back and forth in the Lulworth Cove Pub with a gang of Brits, singing Bobby Dylan. When it was over I asked them if anybody knew "I Dreamed I Saw Joe Hill Last Night," and a girl's lovely voice began to sing it, with only the harmonica and our hearts for accompaniment. When that was over I turned and kissed Emma. It was a very good kiss. We were both sweaty and grimy from two long but different days, but it was still very good.

We were walking back up the ramp to Shirley's.

"How would you get up onto land without being seen?" she asked suddenly.

"What?"

"Like Jock said, your commando thing."

I paused. "Every time I've ever talked about this, the girl has disappeared shortly after. It's a mistake."

"Listen, love, I come from one of the most bloody-minded nations in the history of the world. I'm no fragile flower. It interests me."

I knew better, but it interested me, too, and maybe she was the one who could hear about it and not disappear. "Camouflage is part of it," I said. "Staggered timing. Have you ever been reading or watching TV and seen a mouse from the corner of your eye? They're worth studying. Move quickly, short periods of exposure."

"But we do see them, so how good could that be?"

"Good point. Have you ever seen a camouflaged insect or a chameleon, for example, with movements so slow that our eye isn't alerted? If it is, we look and see what appears to be a branch."

"Yes, but I don't think that's much good, either. Takes too long."

"Not if you have time to kill."

"Oooh, brrr. You're withholding the real secret. Why?"

"So I can see living proof of how very bright you are."

"Giving me an IQ test, are we? Well, we'll pay for that. I failed my A levels, which is why I'm working the bar in a hotel."

"Well, they're wrong. You just passed a much higher test, especially if you can tell me what I'm holding back."

She stopped. I didn't know if she was thinking or showing anger about the way I'd handled this delicate subject. I walked over and put my arm around her waist and she didn't reject it. "I think what would be needed," she said, "is some kind of distraction."

"Yes!" I said with pride and relief. "Misdirection. Doesn't need to be something big like an explosion. Just something small and apparently natural. In movies it's the stone thrown to distract the bad guy. We might do the same. There's some dazzling high-tech stuff now that I never got to use. You could set an explosion down the beach if it was already a hostile situation, but the best way is to pick a place nobody is, come in with a wave, drag your fins behind to cover tracks—at least they won't know how many came up. Of course, Jock has a whole *sporran* bag of tricks. He's something of a guerrilla, too."

"Let's not get on about him again," she said. We stopped at the top of the ramp and looked back at the water, and I remembered how the sea holds and reflects the light that the land will absorb. Emma was playing with the hair on the back of my sweaty neck. "You go shower and I'll do the same. Then I'll come to your room and we'll finish up."

I smiled all the way up the road, holding her hand, letting it go when I had to turn in at Shirley's Bed and Breakfast. About fifteen minutes later, Emma came into my room, undressed, and lay down with me, and it seemed that *this* was really what I sought—not Jock but the missing part of myself that Emma was.

Later she told me, in pillow-talk tones, what had happened.

"I hate to talk about this now," I said, "but I'm guessing you have to work tomorrow."

"If I don't get the sack," she said, nuzzling. "The owner's away, but he'll surely be told that I took the night off with the pub full to go to an*other* pub with you, and if you think this"—she grabbed my "this"—"will remain a secret, you don't know small towns.

"Anyway," she continued. "Here's what I know, or I should say what I saw and what Jock told me was true. He said the big money was in a London bank, but he was waving a good bit of it around and boasting about it and the book. I think he had the book with him, maybe in his room or car, but I never even saw it."

"Were there people there you didn't know?"

"Yes. There are always tourists, and workmen on

summer projects, but there were two that didn't fit in at all."

"Two together? Men?"

"Men but not together unless it was one of your misdirections. Seemed to me they glared at each other."

"Descriptions?"

"One was a medium-sized dark fellow, looked more Mediterranean or Middle Eastern than British. Almost no forehead or chin and shaggy black eyebrows. Curly hair, dark with dark eyes . . . yes, and tattoos. He was wearing a short-sleeved T-shirt and the sleeves covered his upper arms, partly, but he had 'em on his forearms, too."

"Tattoos of what?"

"Hard to tell. You don't want to look long at a man like that, but they looked, some of them, like words he'd put on himself, like somebody with a youth gang or from prison."

"Did he look at all like government, military, intelligence, professional criminal?"

"Not a bit. He looked like the kind of common thief who gets nicked and sent up every time he tries something. Completely lower class, bottom feeder. But he definitely had his eye on Jocko."

"The other guy?"

"Redhead. About the same build as the caveman but a bit slimmer and taller, like maybe five foot nine. He was the one got Jock ranting about Scottish independence, the end of the last colonies, and the rest of that codswallop. Jock was pissed, as we say for drunk. Pissed as a newt, or, in polite company"—she tickled my ribs—"which you ain't, mate, 'nissed as a pewt.' I guess Jock is always pissed, but he was raving that night.

Anybody else try that IRA business round here gets greased for the slide down the ramp—the slide to the tide, they call it. But they loved Jock. He could do no wrong."

"This is important. Did they leave when he did?"

"Absolutely. That's what scared me. I saw it as bad news. I mean Jock seemed to think he had some help coming from that monastery, just from a phone call. He said they knew who he was, which is number one with him. But I don't know if he ever got there."

"You didn't call ahead to warn him?"

"Sure, I would have, but when I looked next morning in my car for the itinerary he'd given me, it was gone."

"Stolen?"

"I'd guess, now. I've looked everywhere for it. The car wasn't locked because, well, even with tourists here in the summer and all, I mean, who'd steal an itinerary? For a literary tour?"

"But you did remember the abbey. That must have been his next stop."

"No, he decided to go to Bath for a jazz concert, then to the abbey. I did get it with a local librarian's help. By then, Jock had already been to Bath, I guess. A Brother Michael came onto the line and said that Jock had checked into their guest-house retreat. He didn't say it, but he implied it was for drying out. But Jock had left the second day at the abbey, before I called. He told the brother that he had to deliver the Granada, but that wasn't where he went. Maybe you can get a copy of the tour from Brother Michael."

"I have one," I said, "from Jock's wife. She and the publisher hired me to find the book."

She paused, colored—pink-red above her perfect white breasts—and said, "That *bas*tard!"

"You're too kind, really. We ain't seen nothin' yet. Did Brother Michael say he'd be following up on the itinerary, assuming Jock gave him one?"

"He didn't say yes or no. He sounded involved, but not completely forthcoming. It's possible."

"How involved are you?"

Her eyes did that guarded thing I'd seen the first moment. It's hard to describe. My heart told me it was righteous anger and suspicion struggling with an effort to be open. My experience told me it was lyin' eyes, holding off forever from commitment, searching for perfect ambivalence, the deniable assertion, the assertive denial, keeping always all options open. Why was I scared and maybe even unfair? Because I was in love. Finally she gave me something: "I don't care what happens to him except so far as it concerns you."

"I feel the same," I said, wishing I could believe her.

Now that I knew Jock knew I was after him and knew that I knew he knew I was after him, how should I adapt? I could think of nothing I should change. I must hit every spot, follow every lead. Jock was always looking for weakness, and he might come back to exploit any he'd seen, should things go wrong elsewhere. But I did call Connie and the editor to ask if they'd heard from him and if that might explain how he knew of me. They both said no. "To have found help and then run!" was Connie's reaction. "The money! The book!" was Ellis's. I filled them both in except for Emma and the two sinister men, so it was mainly a travelogue.

Then I filled Emma in and she emptied me of desire. I love that fleeting empty feeling. Buddha was half right, but never mind Zen; the best cure for desire is someone like Emma. It lasted only about ten minutes and I began to feel desire again, but the cure was still handy, warm, sweet, willing.

NINE

At the T. S. Eliot house in East Coker he'd written:

> Another expatriate. Maybe you and Henry
> and Bob Frost knew best. But I'm not hollow,
> old T.S. (The students called you tough shit
> Eliot, literal sophomores—inevitable.) I'm
> full of juices both fresh and fermented. I eat
> peaches until the juice runs down and unrolls
> my trousers. Actually you were great, like
> Yeats, giving us a lifetime of portentous lines,
> riddles to unlock the human heart. Thanks,
> Old Possum. Please ask God's mercy on the
> Wild Ginger Man.

At Hardy's cottage he wrote:

> Although I hesitate to say this to a man experi-
> encing eternity, life is not so patient as you
> presumed, wasn't even in your own day. How
> long must a man journey to bring home the
> fortune that will no longer win the heart of his
> youth's sweetheart? Why should young Tess,

Old Jude, suffer so much? Why must the *reader* suffer? I see no good in making this sweet land seem so bleak. We already have the Book of Job. I hope you had a little fun before you checked out—seized a few days.
Yours,
  Jock the Soon-to-Be-No-Longer Obscure

Now that might be a clue, I thought, as I drove toward Lynmouth and the Rising Sun. Could he have some plan for which all of this was publicity? From the look of his clear handwriting he was stewed, but not crazy. Could it have to do with the U2 and now the Greenpeace protest near Sellafield, which I thought was over, or with the hippies at Stonehenge? His politics lately wouldn't seem sympathetic to those—different as *they* were.

Did he have a plan to leap from obsolescence to instant world celebrity? Would it risk his life? Had it already taken his life? Or would I check into one of these places soon and see him sitting at the bar? "Slide up here, Gato, have yourself a sarsaparilla or some frog water."

Lynmouth nestled along the banks of the West Lyn River across from Wales and on the north coast of the peninsula that became Cornwall. I was really getting Welsh radio now. Just above Lynmouth on a cliff was a second tourist town, Lynton. A cable car near the water's edge connected them for tourists, and of course roads did so inland. I remembered it fondly from 1986, hunting Mr. Patel and his daughter but one night letting it go and doing some pub singing that MacLeod *didn*'t start, including the song about "The House of the Rising Sun," which was the name of my favorite inn, restaurant, and pub there, though, as at the Castle Inn, my head paid a price for its Tudor charm and dwarfish dimensions.

To get there you drive along the coast through the Exmoor Forest, again suggesting the Pacific coast. I saw more magpies; many sheep; heather; and the great, ugly thistle weeds like those some sentimental Brit had brought to our Pacific coast; more salt-wind-bonsaied conifers; and cattle and sheep guards, though I saw no cattle and the sheep didn't seem to mind crossing the bars and filling the road. It was so much like that peninsula near Woodside, south of San Francisco, that I almost forgot where I was.

My disorientation wasn't helped by the crowds of Americans swarming the Lynmouth streets or by the vans and other movie equipment making a Nescafé commercial.

I knew I'd need Bobby Gaunt with this Scottish nationalism theme confirmed, so I found a slot phone and called him. I saw no way my card could be traced, and it sure helped the spook business not to be toting all that change. In the old days, you could tell a spy by the sound of his pockets. "The eagle [*ca-chang, ca-chang*] flies at ["Please deposit sixty P for three more minutes" —*ca-chang, ca-chang, ca-chang*—"thank you"] midnight."

Bobby was my boat-mate, a Special Air Services early recruit who'd cross-trained with my UDT/SEAL class early in that program at Little Creek, Virginia. That was way back when we weren't even allowed to say it existed. I'd gotten his number after a two-day runaround with the SAS at Hereford when I was here in '86. He was still active duty then with SAS, who'd evolved into missions similar to ours—quick-strike, antiterrorist. They were bodyguards for Salman Rushdie.

Bobby hated swimming underwater or even swimming *in* water, but so did many of us. I was also afraid of heights. One of our mottos became: "A SEAL has nerves; he just ignores them." Bobby might have retired by now, but whatever he was doing he'd be plugged in. You never got completely unplugged from outfits like ours.

You get very close to the five other guys in your training boat. For a week every boat carried a length of telephone pole everywhere. We ran with it; we carried it into the chow hall and ate with it on our laps; and if one of us had to use the head, we all went and stood with him at the urinal or sat on adjoining toilets if possible, with the pole on our laps. Later they substituted a railroad tie, which was heavier and had mean edges and splinters, and was sticky with tar. That wasn't even Hell Week. That kind of close.

I got Bobby on the second ring. He answered: "Sergeant Major Gaunt speaking on a nonsecure phone."

"So you went all the way up," I said. "This is Sierra. On a pay phone."

With no emotion he said to give him my number and he'd call me back. That's the drill.

The phone rang in seven minutes and he was more friendly. "What's the dodge this time, mate? Stealing more of our upright citizens' children, are you? Are we still on the same side?" Bobby had little respect for guys with our training who got out and sold their services to the highest bidder.

"This one's strange, but aren't they all. We're still good guys. Are you active duty?"

"No, old friend. I took mine at twenty-five years. It was that or a desk. I'm doing some training for the U.N. Can't talk about it. Last official job was keeping a famous writer alive with hordes of hashishins out to scimitar him into tiny pieces for shish kebab. Can't talk about that, either."

"Tantalizing, that one," I said, enjoying the British sense of humor, or humour, comparing this conversation with one I might have had with one of the others.

"Remember Cuba?" he asked. "That little job they gave us before they sent me home? Last time I let anyone put my head underwater, by the way."

"Yes, I do." We were testing Marine perimeter security at Guantánamo from Fidel's side of the fence. The question was whether we'd get it from our own jarheads or Castro's militia, but we were lucky and left notes for both sides: *Bang Bang, You're Dead* and *Bang Bang, Ustedes Están Muertos*.

"Of course it never happened," I told Gaunt, "so how could I remember?"

"That was the line," he said. "Secret, reliable, deniable. Now your lads are making feature films and mine show up on the odd documentary for those armchair TV soldiers, such as we're becoming. I don't think I like the new publicity. They told us not to tell anybody what we did. I never told my parents for years. They knew I was in the paras, was all."

"Yeah," I said. "By the time I realized I could talk about it, nobody would believe me."

"When do I get to see how old you've become?"

"Soon. Let me put you onto my problem and maybe

you can ask questions and get answers by the time I head over your way." Gaunt lived east of Cambridge.

"I'm taking notes," he said.

"Another writer, this one American and crazy. How come words are so important these days? Should be a good thing, but everybody's trying to kill the ones who write them. I knew this one after I got out, in college. Lately he disappears over here on a literary tour. A real boozer, but there's more to it than that. He's teasing me now, knows I'm here or guessed I would be. He conned a silly editor out of a million bucks for a book that may be a fraud. Says the money's in a London bank, but I don't know."

"Tarry a bit, Gat," he said. "You know I only read books about sheep and explosives. What good would I do?"

"This guy's been making big Scots nationalist noises since before he left the States. He may have made some contacts, but I know nothing about these people, how serious they are. I assume they connect with the IRA."

"Right, with the harmless ones, the public spokespersons, but the serious Provos are beyond recall, beyond making alliances. They trust nobody they haven't known their whole lives, and then not much. They just killed an MI5 man who'd spent years coming up through the ranks. One of our ops lads went over to them, not a spook but a lad with our training, but I can promise they'll use him and not trust him. It's all quite serious—maybe you heard they blew up Harrod's store in London and the Grand Hotel in Brighton with the Parliament and Prime Minister due to assemble there. Different timing, the whole government gone. Of course, things change, and the thing is to find out. But

I need something—photos, fingerprints, even aliases might help."

"Of course. Just making sure that you're still there."

"Always here for you, mate. Wouldn't mind stretching things a bit for a good cause. Never thought I'd be teaching counterterrorism with slides and a little control button in my hand, waiting for the translators to catch up. Very high tech these days, some of it. Semtex, computer-chip timing fuses, Kevlar, Lexan, fifty-cal bench-rest sniper rifles with heat sensor so you can see through and shoot through a fucking concrete wall—with accuracy! Wouldn't mind a good old-fashioned brawl for a change."

"Wouldn't that clear the head?" I said.

"I'll look into it," he said. "Meanwhile, get me some intel and I'll run your Celtic gentlemen, including the writer."

"Why him?"

"No reason. I'm just suspicious by nature and training."

I gave him everything I could think of on Jock, which wasn't much. I could probably lift some prints off bar glasses if I got close enough. Maybe at the abbey, but they'd probably cleaned up. He hadn't been in the service or in prison, so there may not be prints on him filed anywhere. I didn't know his social security number or even his passport number. No, they must be in that file. I asked Bobby to hold and got them and gave them to him, but they wouldn't be much help now that he was inside the country. He might need the passport for a bank transaction, and Bobby could flag that.

"I'll look into it," Bobby said. "Remember our boat's motto: 'It is better to kill than to be killed.'

Other lads wanted something stronger, but you watered it down with your wishy-washy liberalism."

"Speaking of which," I said. "Riley and Swanker drowned in the Grenada fiasco, and our other, real Cuban, Rodríquez, of a heart attack training contras in Honduras. That's my side. What about our Royal Marine Special Boat Squadron mate, Heald?"

"Bought it in the Falklands. Thought you knew that. Probably took a hundred Argentinian sharpshooters to put one round into him."

"Jesus, Bobby, it's just us left."

"That's why we must look after each other. By the way, those statistics, at our age, might be the same for a group of accountants. At least we had fun and mainly did good."

"Soon," I said, and we rang off.

TEN
◆◆◆◆

LYNMOUTH WAS MAINLY a pleasure, mainly because there was no word of MacLeod. He'd skipped ahead, perhaps to Bath for two or three days, then Downside. I had a conversation down the road at the Bath Hotel Bar. The bartender had been a U.S. Marine and a merc in Africa, had come here for a vacation nineteen years ago and had never gone back to the States. Now he was planning a return home for his English wife and children, to Detroit. I didn't know how to prepare him, so I let it go. He was in for a shock.

I spoke vaguely of "the troubles," but he didn't have much to say about the IRA except that terrorism was terrorism—he'd learned that in Africa working for the big, bad guys who are always the only ones who can hire talent, and would never do it again—and he hoped whoever was bombing for whatever cause wouldn't make another Lockerbie of his family's trip home. I hoped so, too. Seeing Detroit would be enough of a shock.

Back at the Rising Sun, I had my first formal meal of this time in Britain: leg of fresh, local lamb with a mint sauce that was not a sweet jelly but instead ground fresh mint leaves in an almost vinaigrette sauce; a lovely vegetable plate with new potatoes, carrots, green beans, and broccoli; a dessert pudding, mocha and chocolate in light and dark brown, which was really a work of art as well as a perfect light confection; and coffee ranking with the best. They did not serve Nescafé—though the trucks were still parked outside.

I almost asked for a room change because I was on the street side of the second floor and had a couple above me along with the certainty of the commercial crew buses arriving early tomorrow to try to make Nescafé seem like that great real coffee of last night. I regretted not changing because the woman of the couple above found a thousand reasons to pace the floor of the tiny room—apparently rearranging furniture and putting things in drawers for a one-night stay. I never heard her husband's voice, but she kept talking to someone. How could there be that much to say? Maybe he wasn't answering.

Among the enduring mysteries is that of what neighbors are doing to make such odd sounds. I remember Woody Allen's speculation that his upstairs neighbor had to be choking a parrot. After forty some minutes of this woman's maniacal pacing and one-way conversation, and with midnight (and northern nightfall) soon upon us, I knocked on my light bathroom door so it would carry up and called out in what was I hope a moderate voice—if I can hear their pillow talk, surely they could hear this—"Kindly stop choking your parrot."

I heard the man's voice for the first time say, "Sorry." We all fell asleep.

The next day the tide was not full but receded almost

beyond sight. The boats lay in the trickle of the Lyn like children's abandoned toys. The next morning's breakfast seemed to have assembled the entire cast of last night's mystery, so I decided to play Poirot. As I was leaving I asked the waitress in a level but clear voice: "Is there a parrot on the premises?" The breakfast crowd froze into a *tableau vivant*. I looked in from the street for the guilty party, and they were all whispering—not table to table but still confined to isolated suspects. I looked through the window for the one who was not whispering, but then a crewman of the commercial said, "Wanta move it, mate?" and I ambled on. When I had tricked him with my compliance, I walked into his shot, scratching my privates, then packed the Panda, cackling to myself like Herbert Lom as Chief Inspector Dreyfuss when he thinks he's got Clouseau.

It was time to visit Downside. It was a pleasant drive. I'd been disabused of the notion of a perfectly pastoral England on my first trip, so I wasn't bothered much anymore by things like KNAVESBOROUGH TOYOTA or the carefully lettered sign for SNACK'S—a usage I thought confined to the American South. I certainly didn't miss the fast-food joints; the pubs made it all so much more interesting. I did wonder about such phenomena as the MOBIL FISH SHOP TRUCK, but I now knew that signs like RISK OF GROUNDING and BLIND SUMMIT were road warnings, not towns, and that MAJOR PLANT CROSSING did not mean lumbering oaks and redwoods or herds of shrubbery.

I thought the motorway and A road franchise well conceived and executed, if anybody cared for my opinion. I knew that Welcome Break restaurants in the

Forte franchise complexes of petrol, lodging (often with their own restaurants), and buffet-style food were the best places to eat, but the Granada franchise Happy Eater places were okay if you preferred waited tables to buffets, and the Little Chefs weren't bad, either, and could be found on some of the smaller roads. I wasn't sure if I'd try the franchised motels such as that at the Welcome Break on the motorway, because I'd had such good luck with pubs and inns, except for my head.

The question I can never answer is how do they get that one squire in tweed into every pub in Britain? He may be alone or with his lady, but his class is strongly evident; the lines on his face distinct from those you'd find on his working class contemporaries. He always looks to me vaguely like John Kenneth Galbraith.

There was more radio news about the protests near Sellafield. The U2 fans and Greenpeace organizers had skirted a ban on their demonstration by waiting for low tides and walking on sand below the high-tide mark. It confused the constabulary—riparian rights and all—much as they'd been confused by squatters' claims on the "sacred" lands near Stonehenge, Avebury, and in some locales where those wondrous, large, ancient chalk designs had been drawn by perhaps those same beaker people, of warriors with swords raised and erect penises. Of course the government preserved those sites for obvious and good reasons, but until recently—ancient law about property curiously being a more open issue here—they had had trouble finding grounds to expel the unsightly visitors.

No nonsense this year. Iron Lady Thatcher was gone, but her legacy was to be seen in a heavy police cordon around the monuments until after the solstice. A spokesman for nearby landowners said, "Half that lot couldn't tell you what a solstice is, much less what it means in their so-called religion. To me their religion is bein' lazy and usin' drugs and actin' ugly for attention." Earlier I'd gotten another view from a guy on my telly—having browsed a bit at Lynmouth waiting for the parrot to die—who called himself the Lowatollah of Britain. He declared that he would lead the righteous followers of "white magic," ancient pagan wisdom, and modern "green consciousness" past the police cordon. He said a spell was in the making that would raise police consciousness while lowering police vigilance. He seemed to be trying to be Britain's Timothy Leary or Ken Kesey, but it didn't play well. Under his "Druidic" robe and various chains with arcane symbols and his large, thick, black-framed, tinted glasses, he looked like a dentist or chiropractor.

There seemed to be a small cottage industry of those pretending to lead and speak for movements that had begun in the United States, a kind of reversal of Twain's Dauphin and Duke of Bilgewater. There was a faith healer packing them in who claimed to have healed the U.S. and was now offering his gift to the U.K. I'd never heard of him, but the British press were taking him seriously. It hadn't occurred to anyone to make a few phone calls to New York or L.A. This guy's name was Cirullo or something close to that, and the pity was that he might make his fortune on just this one trip unless the public caught on and gave him the send-off it gave the Duke and Dauphin after their Royal Nonesuch performance. Could the benighted clods of Missouri and Arkansas be smarter than the modern Brits? Suddenly I thought: Is this something like what MacLeod's doing?

ELEVEN
◆◆◆◆

THE ABBEY WAS beautiful, not ancient but a tasteful neo-Gothic with what I took to be flying buttresses supporting the choir. The boys' school next door was in an undistinguished brick building that did not compete. What did seem odd was the basketball backboard and net being against a wall just behind and so close to the abbey's south door that the monks, should they wish, could come out dribbling and run a layup drill after matins.

When Brother Michael joined me, I mentioned the "holy hoop," and he said that while it was there for the boys, the monks had come to like it for exercise, too. This Benedictine order was mainly contemplative with the other job of teaching, so they needed exercise that some of their other co-religionists got in the field.

"Jock's in a bad way, wouldn't you say?" I hoped the sudden shift to the real subject might make him turn over the ball if he had it.

"Very much so," he said. "Would you like to shoot a few?"

Brother Michael was better at the game than I, and he wasn't a bad basketball player, either. The game was really Jocko and what to do about him. We talked as we warmed up and began what became a very competitive game of one-on-one.

"Make it, take it?" I asked.

"Inner-city rules. Fine."

"You rather play Loser?" In that version, the guy who makes the shot lets the other guy take it back and try his game.

"No, your Winner game's fine with me. Play the rim?"

"Yeah." That meant if you shot, you'd better hit the rim or your opponent could get it and put it up without taking it back behind the top of the key. If you at least hit the rim, he had to take it back before he could shoot, and you had a chance to defend.

"Free throw for who goes first?" he asked.

"You go," I said, which wasn't so much gentlemanly as a kind of playground macho psychology—you don't worry me.

I had height on him to spare, but he was fast, and he didn't seem to recognize or wasn't able to admit a foul. I was playing with a bad knee and no brace and as what I'd been on the court years ago: a hacker, a foul specialist who's also good enough to make it look like an awkward accident. What Phil Jackson was to the old Knicks and Bill Laimbeer was to the more recent championship Pistons. I came down with an elbow to the shoulder point that deadened Brother Michael's shooting arm long enough for us to take a break and redefine the game, and let us talk.

"Sorry," I said. "Clumsy of me."

He just laughed and looked up at both our judges, the Great Referee. "Jock said you were tough."

"How tough is he? I mean, how much more of this self-abuse can he stand? He has to quit drinking. Agreed?"

"Yes, and I hope he's ready, but he's all jangled up with this Scots business and trying to be a Catholic and worrying about his literary reputation, anything but facing the problem and dealing with it."

I didn't know we were still playing, so it surprised me when he drove past me for a layup. I rebounded and let him take it back. "Will he convert?" I asked, knowing it would occupy part of his mind.

"I won't instruct him until he's been sober for at least six months."

"Are you a priest as well as a monk?"

"All of us are here."

"Do you have a satellite dish? I mean, you do have a basketball hoop."

"Yes, actually, hidden behind the trees. Why?"

"Have you ever caught the Sisters of Celes—"

"Yes, our favorite. Really a wonderful ministry. We especially love Sister Sarah. We were even thinking of doing a plainsong video, you know, 'Greatest Gregorian Hits,' but they're probably much too hip."

"Don't second-guess them. Do it. Send it to Sister Sarah, care of the Order, Russian Island, Washington. Mention me."

"You're kidding." He was really excited.

"I'm not without influence there."

"Are you a Catholic?"

"Don't let the Spanish name fool ya. My family has a lapse the size of the Grand Canyon."

"Protestant?"

"Zen Wobbly," I said.

"Wobbly?"

"I.W.W. Anarcho-syndicalist."

"Oh, right, of course."

He was careless and I stole it from his dribble and took it back. I drove as if to come over him, then pulled up for a fadeaway jumper that missed, but did hit the rim. He laughed and took it back. "Although he insists on calling me his confessor, so I guess"—he faked left and came around to his right, then turned and backed into me hard, faked to his and my left, then went right and caught me with a left-hand shot I didn't know he had—"that I'm bound to keep anything he tells me confidential." He took the ball back. "That's why you're so important." I knew he was coming with that ego teaser, driving right into me with his left shoulder, then starting to spin back to our right for another leftie. I just grabbed and held him.

"Foul," he said.

"Playground rules," I said. "Why am I so important?"

He smiled and tossed it up underhanded, and it went in. "Because you're the only one he knows who's given up the sacred nectar and still seems to have any fun or attract any admirers."

"What's to be done?" Our game was over.

"Nothing unless he's done," he said. "If I had him here and he could get a few sober months behind him, well . . . but you know yourself that a man or woman has to hit bottom, and he just hasn't."

"How deep can his bottom be? He's been bouncing off it for years, trying to dig it deeper. He revels in it. How does he stay alive? I've got to confess I expect it of him, admire it in some perverse way. I didn't know that until just now."

"It does seem," Michael said, "that his generation have a longer run at it than we younger ones."

"Where do you suppose he is?"

He looked away and nodded his head. "It'd be hard to know."

"This I know," I said, still wondering about how carefully he'd chosen his last words. "He was last seen at Drumnadrochit. There's no word of him any farther along his planned tour."

"That's what I've been told."

"We haven't mentioned his pursuers. He must have told you about them."

Brother Michael went to retrieve the ball. For the first time it struck me how odd it was to be playing basketball with a monk in his habit. "Lord, what would Nike do with this," I said, and it wasn't lost on him.

"Spike Lee and I one-on-one," he said, and we laughed. "We tried to recruit Christian Laettner to the order—we could cream the Dominicans, anybody with a guy like that. But while his name was Christian, he wasn't prepared to give up the N.B.A. I'm just kidding."

"You're pretty worldly yourself," I said. "Did you tell him he could have big-time adventures in between sessions of plainsong?"

"Seriously," he said. "There's one development you may not know about. By the time he got here, the manuscript had been stolen. He said he was mugged at Bath, but he wouldn't say more."

"So he changed his itinerary?" I asked. "He was scheduled to come here first."

"Yes, he went to hear jazz, the Bobby Wellins, Jim Mullen Quintet, and they got him there. If only he had come here first. With the book here, he might have stayed. Maybe he thought that if they sent you after him and he was still missing, you'd be more likely to find the book, too."

"Do you think they have Jock?"

He did an involuntary head fake, then said, "They wouldn't need him if they have the book, would they? A book's less trouble and less illegal than kidnapping, holding a man."

"But the 'they' are two competing factions or individuals. They want different things, and we don't know what yet. At least I think they are from my only description of them—I make one as criminal, one political."

"Often the same these days," he said. "Then we must hope to hear soon. I think he really did lose the manuscript—or in this setting, to be accurate, typescript. Whether it was legitimate, what kind of book it was, I don't know."

"Ah, but you suspected on your own that it might be a forgery, plagiarism, some kind of fraud."

"Perhaps, but I think it meant something to him, whatever it was, and I doubt those who grabbed it know its true value. He lost some money, too, but he seems to have put most of it into some bank. He wouldn't say which."

"I can't believe that as a professional writer he doesn't have a copy stashed away, maybe at that same bank."

"Worth checking, but somehow it seemed crucial to him that it be the only copy. Why?"

"Because if it left his hands, someone might spot the fraud?" That was my instinct. "Or he might have a copy but will never tell where. Maybe in the States. Two men follow him from Lynmouth," I said, "but they don't seem to be together. One seems very respectful of Jock's pan-Celtic diatribe, but that doesn't mean he couldn't have brought him into dangerous company. People start things they can't finish. I call the dark one the Pict and the red-haired idealist the Scot."

"So there might be a blackmail note? We need to be sure there's a way for them to contact somebody. They may not know about me. Jock mentioned a girl at West Lulworth, Emma. Might they contact her?"

"I hope not," I said. "I've left cards and numbers everywhere I could. They should find me soon, I hope. But I'll check in with Emma, too. I'll go to Bath next. Maybe that's where they're looking for a contact." I paused. I thought of something. "Is it possible that Jock's a true believer, a bagman for the IRA or SRA or whatever, who not only rips off his publisher but has the public excuse of having it 'stolen' by terrorists?"

"Listen to what you're saying," said Brother Michael. "I've known him only a short time, but I can tell you he won't give much of anything to anybody, except promises. Idealism? Self-sacrifice? And how long have you known him?"

"Lost my head," I said. We sat on the chapel steps, facing the green wood. The boys were playing somewhere out of sight. "Unless he could figure a way to double-scam, somehow make more on it than the first hoax—I may be losing it here, but a movie deal, something. Or maybe he was forced to do this all along, blackmail, a death threat to Connie. Never mind that. I . . ."

Brother Michael seemed moved, and I didn't have a clue why. "You love the man in some way," he said.

"I hate him. He's the Inspector Clouseau to my Inspector Dreyfuss. I wouldn't mind giving him the deep six in the Irish Sea."

"Deeper down than that," he said, "and you can't imagine that he could ever suffer enough to break."

"I . . ." He had me there. "I can't imagine *him* . . ." I couldn't talk, ambushed by the whole thing for the first time.

"Think of how many years," Michael said, "his pride in you. Your pride—admit it—in him. Love's not rational. It's very often not even kind or decent. You are here to overthrow your father, Randall, and at the same time you dread doing it. Not your real father— that may be resolved satisfactorily—but your, what, spiritual father?"

I wanted to tell him what a load of Emma's codswallop that was, but I still couldn't talk, so I got up and began walking to my car.

"Something else," he called after me. "He may not succeed, but he's trying to make his last large statement here and now. If it isn't written in a book, who's to say that the accumulated media record isn't as valid? He sees himself as the Gaelic *sennaiche*, the storyteller, but also as one of the epic heroes of the tales—a great naked Celt, fighting and singing to his last breath. All I'm saying is, have some sympathy for him, and recognize that you care."

"He's pulled the kilt over your eyes, too," I said.

"Watch out for the dirk beneath. These Scots are famous for inviting people to dinner and then killing them—one big happy, bloody family. Remember Macbeth. Thanks for the game. I needed the exercise."

TWELVE
◆◆◆◆

THERE'S NOTHING LIKE a bath after a game of hoops, and I was headed there anyway, where the Romans used to wash away the grime and stress of empire. It's one of my favorite places, Bath (pronounced "Baath"), more exotic than a movie lot yet comfortable, user-friendly, a city that abruptly becomes countryside at its edges, with no suburban sprawl, convenience stores, car dealers, burger joints. Just one minute you're on a street of lovely Georgian homes and the next you're over a fence and into a field. Bath also suggests the Romans more than any other active English city, and somehow I find that reassuring.

When I travel I carry saxophone mouthpieces, always an alto and baritone and sometimes a tenor. Carrying the whole horn is impractical, and this way, if I find a group playing jazz, especially one with a serious reed man, I can offer a sanitary augmentation of their horns, if he uses one and gives me another, or a substitution, if the reed man wants to take a break. I carry neck straps, too. Of course I have to be able to play, but so far nobody's pushed me off the stand, and I got paid for a week not long ago in Brazil—in Rio, not someplace up the Amazon.

I'd taken the lodgings that MacLeod had used, and it was the first time I wasn't hearing horror stories. I heard so little about MacLeod, in fact, from Mrs. Avis (a perfect name for Bath) that I used his photo for the first time, to see if it had been a well-behaved impostor. "That's our poor Mr. MacLeod," she said. She showed it to her husband in his chair and he nodded confirmation.

"I take it you didn't have too much trouble with him," I asked.

"He had trouble enough without giving us any. Poor man was robbed of his great book, right here, not two blocks away. Very sad."

Another MacLeod strategy. God knew he'd used it often enough on Connie. He could project such genuine hurt that the very stones—and Bath had more than its share—would weep. Any novice writer knew to keep a copy, and whatever that book actually was, I knew Jock had several tucked away.

But maybe he had been mugged, and that can make the strongest of us feel vulnerable, certainly more frail and human than Old Jocko wished to feel. And he'd tried to dry out, I assumed, with Brother Michael, also Father Michael, also a pretty good shooting guard. Jock had tried to face sobriety and panicked, so of course he was down. And Michael was right that I was having trouble imagining Jock defeated, even retreating. I guess that *is* the idea of the father that must be overthrown: his invincibility.

"Did he do anything unusual besides losing the book?"

"I can't think of anything," she said. "You know we're having the jazz festival and he was here for some of that. It goes all summer, though not every night." I already knew there was a quintet playing tonight, with some names I remembered from the old Ted Heath and Johnny Dankworth with Cleo Lane bands.

"There *was* the healing service," Mr. Avis said. "That's unusual, isn't it? He seemed disappointed by that. Is he ill?"

I thought it over and said, "Yes."

"Pity," he said. "Perhaps he'll get better."

I knew what would make me feel better. I took a hot bath, then dressed. I had all three mouthpieces in my jacket pocket and an umbrella because it finally looked like rain, and I headed down to town. I ate at a fair French restaurant and found the concert hall in a complex of rooms built above the baths themselves. Good jazz would drive away the blues.

This group was in a groove from 1945 to 1965, when jazz hit its peak. It was just what I wanted to hear, and listening to Dizzy Gillespie's "Night in Tunisia" above the remains of a Roman bathhouse is among the memories I hope will flash before me when I die. It seemed that our culture had continuity, made sense, maybe even including MacLeod. Jazz can be very strict with its performers, but its spirit in the audience is usually very Catholic; everybody belongs, we all understand, all is forgiven.

The sax player led the group, so I was even more hesitant to approach than usual, but I went up after the first set and explained my situation, and asked if they'd be playing anywhere after hours. It was strange hearing hip argot in a Scottish brogue: "This is not infallible, because you may know all and not be a player, like that old sot, that American who wanted to sing scat a while ago, or know naught and be a natural, but it's a test I use, so please tell me who wrote 'Dat Dere.' "

"I think it was Bobby Timmons, who also wrote the waltz 'Dis Here' "—I gave it the full black "Dis Hyunh" sound. "Oscar Brown, Jr., wrote the vocalese lyrics for 'Dat Dere' and recorded it. Cannonball did, too—record it, I mean."

"Vocalese lyrics is redundant," said the Scottish tenor man, pronouncing it *redoondant.* "But you're close enough for jazz. Come in for a number, take eight bars. If I nod, take twenty-four more. If you're cuttin' it, ye can stay for three numbers. I usually play tenor, so you can play alto or bari."

"If we'll be staying with this Miles, Cannonball, Monk material, the alto would be more authentic."

"Aye, and more obvious if ye foock oop."

"I'm hip."

"I hope so."

I don't know how to say this other than stating that the idea of the Roman baths beneath somehow put me at ease, and I played the best alto I've ever played. I imagined Emma hearing it, and even Jock. We did "Well You Needn't," "Milestones," and a rousing gospel-flavored version of "Mercy," and they surprised me by asking me to stay on for the last three numbers. When they told me what they'd be playing, I switched to baritone, and we did some West Coast–sounding numbers: "Line for Lyons," "But Not for Me," and "Midnight Sun," perfect for this season in the north.

I was walking home in perfect contentment, my mouthpieces still warm in my jacket pocket and my umbrella still folded, almost to the Avis house, when two men stepped from between buildings and one of them said, "Word wiv you, guv."

But the other made the mistake of moving close on my right, trying, I thought, to get behind me. Without thinking, I brought the umbrella handle down on his nose, then hooked it under his crotch and encouraged him—his legs seeking purchase in the air, not wanting the points of the wrought-iron pickets but wanting even less the hook coming up hard under his scrotum. Over he went, crashing into the dark well where garbage cans are kept.

"Wait now," the other said. I'd had him in peripheral vision and took his movement toward me the way I'd been trained to take it in the proverbial dark alley, stepping aside, grabbing his lead right arm with my right hand, which still held the umbrella, turning it to torque and full extension, then breaking it with a heel of palm strike to his barred elbow. I used the umbrella to help him over the fence to join his friend. Even as he fell, he made a sound that I finally understood as a piteous wail not just of a mugger who's been hurt but of someone whose behavior and intent have been misunderstood, and I knew he was right.

Both men were thrashing around and yelling in pain. I knew now that they'd approached to give me a chance to buy back MacLeod's book. They weren't very good at what they were doing, and I was too good. I thought of helping them out. I knew the second was my Pict, and maybe he was stupid enough to be carrying ID and I could snatch it before a crowd gathered. His mate was probably recruited from a seedy London pub for a one-night job. But no, the light had gone on in the house on whose garbage cans they were thrashing and the coppers would soon be here. I didn't want official strings attached to me at this point, so I leaned down and said, "Next time don't come at me that way. I'll buy the damned book back."

I heard the Pict wail, "You broke me arm, you brut-al bastard. You didn't 'ave to do that."

It was time to go. I ran down to the Avises' door and opened it. I couldn't tell from what I heard in the street whether they got away or not. They might be telling the police that they'd just been mugged. As I swung the door open I heard the slightest honk of a horn. I looked across the street and saw a van. The driver opened his door briefly so the interior light would show him to me. I figured he was the Scot. He gave me a thumbs-up sign, closed his door, started his engine, and sped away. I didn't do everything wrong. This time I got his tag number.

The Pict would get his arm fixed down the road, and I'd have to wait for him to contact me again. It now seemed possible that the Pict and his buddy had Mac-Leod somewhere and that my trained overreaction meant he'd stay there longer, perhaps weeks longer. I didn't want to be getting his fingers and earlobes. But I didn't figure the Scot would let that happen. He might not be able to get the novel back and he might not know MacLeod's whereabouts, but he seemed now to have a good tail on the Pict Gang. Come to think of it, the Pict Gang probably didn't have MacLeod, or they wouldn't be dealing with me. Unless MacLeod refused to talk, and he wasn't that brave. Unless they knew MacLeod was dead and I didn't. No, wouldn't the Scot have warned me? Maybe he was committed to tailing them for the book, but he could have yelled across: "Mac-

Leod's dead." That phrase stayed with me in fitful sleep. Mr. Avis was having an ulcer attack upstairs, or gas, they didn't know which, because "You know I can't eat cabbage, yet you served it."

"But you ate it. Nobody forced you."

I wondered how long that argument had been going on, how many decades. It was that kind of blame-filled night. I should have been hearing Cannonball's solo on "Milestones." Instead, I spent the night with the Bickering Avises and my own shame and blame for overreacting, and the phrase "MacLeod is dead." When I slept, I dreamed I'd killed him, shot him twice in the chest and once in the head—the old Mozambique Triple Tap—for reasons that had been exposed before I came into the dream. So I stood over him with a smoking gun, thinking: God, I wish this were a dream. I was grateful when the Avises woke me with a little morning replay of who was to blame for the Gas Attack.

I checked the morning Bath paper for names of the victims, but there was nothing. I went out after breakfast and called Bobby Gaunt from a pay phone, then waited for him to call me back. This time it was ten minutes. A different booth, perhaps. "Can you run this separatist guy's van tag," I asked, "without setting off claxons and SWAT teams?"

"I can try. They understand that I do private consulting, but if he's been active they may ask me what's up. I told you this was serious business."

"Maybe we should hold off," I said, "because he's doing me a big favor now and I don't want to get him nicked, as you people say."

"Why not give me the number and I'll hold on it? If

something should happen to you, I'd be bound to get them and I'd have a lead."

I hesitated. This feud was centuries old, between the English and the Celts, and in that time had only gotten worse. Bobby had lost friends to the IRA, and to them he was just another Black and Tan with a blue or red or sand-colored beret. And if he was really freelancing, how did I know for whom? This took too long and we both knew it.

He tried to give me a way out. "Or just give it to me when you have more. The van's probably stolen anyway."

"How'd you know it was a van?"

"Steady on, mate, you told me it was a bloody van."

I couldn't let this happen. There had to be a fulcrum of trust somewhere, and if it didn't hold, it was better to be dead from falling off than alive in a world in which you could trust no one. I gave him the tag number.

"Use your discretion," I said. "Keep in mind that he's tailing the worst character, probably the book thief and possibly the kidnapper of MacLeod. And he watched my back last night when I tangled with the other and his mate."

"You're beginning to talk like a Brit," Bobby said. "I don't know what kind. An American movie Brit, perhaps."

"Sound anything like Michael Caine playing a German officer?" I asked, running with the dialect riff. "The man's amazing. He can play anything as a Cockney and somehow we don't care. And Connery, aye, there's a man."

"Not up to either of their standards," Bobby said. "Do I get to hear about the action?"

"They approached me on the street, to demand a ransom for the book, I think, but they came too fast and I switched into automatic."

"You really must invite me to the next one. I think of it the way a geezer thinks of his cricket days or his first woman."

"Yes, it was nice, and yes, I'll try, and Bobby, sorry about the hesitation."

"I understand. It's sad but true. Treachery is commonplace, and the power boys buy and sell and trade us players as if it *were* football. I might have done the same. Call me in a few days. I'll have something. Unless he's out to kill the queen, I think I can keep it a private job I'm doing and not let slip the dogs of war, or whatever that line is."

"I'll be in Stratford-on-Avon next, the Stratford Inn."

"Coincidence. An old para C.O. of mine runs the place, Clive Davis. Very fine gentleman, and understands the work we're in, though he's not active and spends all his time with his true love, Shakespeare. Tell him hullo, my respects."

I thanked him and called Emma. I'd wanted to before but didn't want her to think me too desperate.

"I've gotten the sack," she said. "I've given notice, or rather been given notice, but"—she stopped talking and I knew the boss was nearby—"yes, *sir*, we're happy to hear our services pleased you."

"Did they ever," I said, and she didn't speak. "Just listen," I said. "Tell him to piss off and meet me in Stratford-on-Avon. Do you have enough money for a day or two?"

"Yes, sir," she said.

"Check in anywhere but the Stratford Inn. Wait, do you even want a job? You could just travel with me."

"I'm afraid not, sir. We can't accept gratuities."

"Independent, are we? Well, then, I'll just have to get you a job at the Stratford Inn."

"That would be very nice, sir, and thank you."

"Leave your number at the desk there, but use another name. What shall it be? Maid Marian, Fergie, Twiggy . . ." I could hear her trying not to laugh. "Ann Boleyn, Mrs. Malaprop, no, Juliet, Tina Brown, Tess of the D'Urbervilles?"

"That's the one, sir."

"Tess, is it? Just say Tess called and leave the number."

Her boss must have moved away because she said, "You fit inside me perfectly, absolutely fill me. I felt afterwards as if I would never be able to move again. I've thought of little else. . . . Yes, *sir*, thank *you*." And she hung up.

I called Bobby again. "I think you can stay home on this one." He said to go ahead slowly. "Your friend . . . around the Globe?"

"Affirmative."

"A very worthy woman needs a part."

"I'll call you soon," he said, and I waited. Loose lips sink ships. Six minutes this time before the phone rang. "Sounded too specific," he said.

"Okay, a lady I love named Emma Poole, with training and experience, needs a job in hotel management. She's bright and beautiful, and she'd have good recs from her last job at the Castle Inn in West Lulworth if the manager hadn't thought she was a milkmaid and himself a lord with sexual percs."

"Wanted to poke her regular, did he?"

"*Exactement.*" I was lying, but it was for a good cause.

"I'll call Clive Davis. You have her call him tomorrow or later, but not too late. Any others—relatives, unemployed friends?"

"No, just her. Thanks again."

"Can't wait to meet her."

"Nor can I. Adios, compadre."

"Ciao," Gaunt said, and hung up.

THIRTEEN

◆◆◆◆

THE STRATFORD INN was on Sheep Street, near the Royal Shakespeare Theatre complex and just around the corner from the Dirty Duck, a theatrical pub, with Shakespeare's birthplace about a block or so in the other direction and the Hathaway cottage about a mile along a public footpath to the fourth, or northwest, corner. It's as good a job of integrating historical significance with tourism as I've seen, and somehow it even made sense to see the schools of Japanese tourists shoot up their rolls of 35 millimeter. Especially when their bus was waiting in the convenient car park nearby and by nightfall they would have snapped Avebury Circle, most of Oxford, and some of Cambridge in late twilight before pouring into the Welcome Break for tea, dinner, and maybe a sitcom before bedtime.

Clive Davis was one of those people who makes you feel immediately and genuinely comfortable. He was bald and ruddy with a fringe of gray hair that grew heavily down his neck. He was one of those men who make no effort to disguise the hairy glories of middle age: His ears and nostrils sprouted hair and his eyebrows were the equivalent of any Russian's. We had the small service bar to ourselves. "Understand you're one of Sergeant Major Gaunt's mates from, well, where our hot wars stopped and your cold one began. He's a rare one, somehow both rock solid and unpredictable. One of the very best, a legend among . . . those who know of such things."

"Sergeant Major," I said. "Highest rank bestowed on an elisted man."

"Nearly didn't get it," Davis said, "because so much of what he's done for a long time is classified. One of the Colonel Blimp types on the board asked him, 'If you can't tell us what you did in all this secrecy, Sergeant Gaunt, can you at least point to a result or two that we wouldn't have if not for you,' and Bobby said, 'Your life, sir, and the lives of those in your family,' and the man turned pale and nearly fainted. And of course it was true, specifically true, the man had been a target and they disarmed the threat without alarming him. No more questions. Bobby lives at the point," he said. "He *is* the point."

"I couldn't describe him better," I said. "I doubt the Bard could."

"Mind your talk about the Bard, here," he said.

"Bobby said you were a—"

"—a student and admirer, and a passionate defender. Do you know that Ben Jonson said that Shakespeare's plays lacked art?"

"Which would seem," I offered, "to prove that Shakespeare was who we think him to be. Where was it recorded?"

"Jonson visited the Scottish poet Drummond, and Drummond wrote it in his diary. Jonson walked all the way from London to Hawthornden Castle, near Edinburgh, on a bet. Drummond was said to have a prodigious wine cellar. Pity Ben didn't keep walking north and freeze on the moors."

"That's what my friend, MacLeod, seems to have done."

"There's a mess," he said, "though I can't say I didn't enjoy him. I'll fill you in, but first, Bobby says you've a good prospect for staff."

"I believe so. I wouldn't have asked Bobby—"

"Not at all. It happens I'm looking for someone, behind the bar first, but definitely career path. Have her come see me soonest."

"Thank you. Now what of MacLeod?"

"You'd better have another Schwepps in preparation. There, that's better. Never touch anything else myself."

"I think I'm ready," I said, "but people have been saying that about MacLeod since I've known him."

"I think I understand," Davis said. "Now for the radio incident I'll have to refer you to Inspector Talley, who dealt with it. I did go his bail for several reasons. The adolescent in question had deliberately put his boom box, as they call them, down next to Shakespeare's birthplace, to provoke something less than he got, I'm sure, but he got what he deserved."

"What did he get?"

"MacLeod snatched the thing away and smashed it onto the sidewalk. That might have been it had the owner not rushed at MacLeod in one of those doped tantrums they can have, so where bodily assault was concerned, the boy struck first, though the magistrate found that MacLeod bore some large responsibility for provoking it. The issues remaining were damage to property, namely the radio, and personal injury to the boy, whom MacLeod ran some three times like a battering ram against the Bard's birthplace before the boy lost consciousness. Witnesses testified that MacLeod said, 'There, maybe some of *that* will rub off,' then, realizing that some blood from the youth's scalp remained on the building, exclaimed: 'My God, what have I done? What defilement, sacrilege!' "

All through this Clive Davis had been in a kind of legalistic style, but he could no longer hold back his joy and delight and—though he covered his mouth like a schoolboy giggling in class—his laughter. When I started laughing, he let his go, and you would have thought we were drunk from soda. Davis tried several times to talk, but couldn't.

"Wish . . . loved . . ."

I had an idea what he was after.

"Would have paid to see it," I finally managed.

Davis was trying so hard to speak through his hilarity that he swept his bottle and glass onto the floor and gripped the bar like a drowning sailor, gasping for breath. But the crash of glass gave him a moment of relative gravity that allowed him to say: "Wish . . . I'd done it myself. Taking shit from those silly . . . green-haired mutants all these years." He wound down and we were both wiping our eyes with bar napkins. "Yes, although I was also motivated by some responsibility since he was a guest here, it did me a world of good. I may do it myself one day." He got out a new glass and bottle, with ice, and poured it, and we fizzled down with the bubbles in his glass.

"That's one thing I'll admit he's good for," I said.

"He sows the seeds of anarchy, does the things that most of us want to do but don't dare."

"Next time," said Davis with some gravity, "I might. Yes, you put it well. He does have great value. The Oxford Union got a taste, too. I don't know what he said, but they heard he was here and invited him, though the term's almost over or perhaps it is, it's been so long since I was. . . . Anyway, they'll have to tell you about that, but *I* have a copy of MacLeod's interruption of *Romeo and Juliet* right here in the Royal Shakespeare Theatre production, directed by . . . well, he's suffered enough.

"By coincidence, that performance was being video-taped for sale to patrons—something I've helped them manage, which is how I got this bootleg copy of something Mr. Better Remain Nameless ordered destroyed. When MacLeod stood and began his tirade, the camera-person naturally shifted to him, as did the lighting crew, by instinct for where the real performance is. So it is preserved. I must swear you to secrecy."

"I'm good at that. So sworn. What was Jock incensed about in particular?"

"Well," Davis began, savoring every word, "he'd just been fined and released, and when I declined to serve him more liquor, he'd gone down to the Dirty Duck and gotten pissed for the play. He already had tickets. What set him off in general was literally the setting. It was one of those mod versions with motor-bikes, switchblades, and all. I know Shakespeare took the same liberties, and I understand doing a kind of *West Side Story* production can refresh the palate now and then, but MacLeod had just been through the radio travesty, and he snapped."

"And?"

"I won't tell you," he said, as happy a man as I'd seen in a long time. "I'll *show* you. Come."

We grabbed extra soda and he filled an ice bucket, and we went to his quarters like thieves who hadn't yet counted their take.

There was no way I could have prepared myself for the sight and sound of MacLeod in this audience, rising up like mad Lear. I'd forgotten the sheer force of his presence. He was clearly a better actor than anyone working on stage beyond the footlights, and the audience, camerapersons, and lighting techs knew it and reacted as if he were part of the play, as well he should be in some version. *That* would refresh the palate.

When he knew he had his audience, he said, "This is a travesty. You're a load of spoiled fruits who've fallen out of the crate, off the wagon. Or a cargo cult worshiping the crate in which Will once lived, with no sense of what was *alive* there."

That Jock was way off the wagon was as obvious in his weaving, hypnotic stance (will he stay up?) as in his metaphors, which tangled themselves together like cats fighting. But none of that detracted from his voice, nor from his bizarre dignity and magnetism.

"I've decided to help you kill this play, put the quietus on this tormented creature." He was mixing plays, too, but nobody laughed. "At least we will no longer be profaning Shakespeare's language, because I've anticipated where all your trendy, silly thinking will take you, and I give you now 'Rappin' Romeo,' to which I retain all rights, the fact that I haven't thought it up yet to the contrary notwithstanding." His last word was a bit mushy in his mouth. Was he up to it? The audience seemed to think so. An excited murmur ran through it. "I am, by the way, for the benefit of the benighted, the writer Jock MacLeod. If I should pay the ultimate price for this effort to defend our greatest poet—the viciousness of these stage sillies is not to be underestimated—I wish to be buried in Westminster Abbey." Nobody laughed. "Even if I'm not killed here, I wish it," he continued, "provided, of course, that I'm dead." Now the audience did laugh.

And they gave him a big hand, as if the curtain had just gone up. He looked at the camera and gave his best ragged, gap-toothed, irresistible grin. Then he snapped his fingers, counting off four, three, two, one, like the leader of a jazz ensemble.

"There be two gangs banging in this old-timey Hood,
 Like the Crips and Bloods, and dig, that ain't good
 For this Romeo homey of the Montagues,
 'Cause the funky sisters he can have is *old* news.
 He be jammin' 'bout Juliet, a Capulet,
 Which mean dissin' her homeys, so it ain't over yet."

We could see the director clawing his way toward the camera, trying to get his hand over the lens, but he was repelled by members of the crew. The camera held on MacLeod as he continued and as the director tried desperately to reach him. It was not necessary for MacLeod to touch the director (he could have broken him in half) because the audience was now with MacLeod and made a human wall around MacLeod like Jacobite loyalists around Bonnie Prince Charlie—who from renderings I've seen was even less bonnie than the hairy, ragged MacLeod. You knew it was over when the orchestra began providing rap percussion. The director was carried away over the heads of the audience, now a mob—the poor man's rage now paled to fear, his eyes wide, his throat too dry and choked with fear to call for help.

MacLeod was making a parody of the bent-wrist rap hand circle, which was itself a copy of Rocky's friend Paulie, a white character played by Burt Young. The expression "Yo" came right out of *Rocky* the original, which came from Philly Italian street slang, which has been falsely claimed by black street rappers and offered as authentic black street argot by short people with short memories like Spike Lee. So this was a cultural circle that MacLeod had put into the air, a hoop, a wheel of juggled objects, a Möbius strip—Renaissance Italian, an attempt at contemporary Italian, African American, Italian American—of conflict and mannerisms.

The last lines I remember—though I must get a copy of the tape—were:

"Hey, yo, yonder window, what light come breakin'?
Check it out, Sunny Juliet, girl, what's shakin'?"

How could he do this? It was a kind of twisted masterpiece. How could he do something like this and not write a great book or play a great Lear or Richard? Was this performance art that would someday enter the canon? Did Jock even know what performance art was? Sure, he'd been paying attention, a furtive MTV voyeur. Yes, now I had a glimmer. His life was, as others had told me, his art. I hated admitting it, but I was impressed.

The last thing I heard him say was "This is dedicated to Emma," and it gave me a chill.

FOURTEEN
◆◆◆◆

IT WAS LATE afternoon when I saw Inspector Talley. It was one of those cop houses at which all business is conducted at a window, like paying your electric bill. As if someone would want to break into a police station, which, come to think of it, will probably be in tomorrow's headlines. I remembered there was a movie about just that—two, come to think of it.

He never invited me in, but he was polite.

"Perhaps the Salvation Army can help you find him, but it sounds as if you're better able to track him, because he won't stand still. Even though he's broken the law, he's paid the price and can't be held. Even though I agree with you that he might be a danger to himself—and I did hear reviews of his performance as well as requests that he be prosecuted—I can't hold him simply because people want me to. I've long felt that some people need or at least want to be lost, and they've that right. We have a long tradition of law, including the right not to like a play. Sometimes the tradition makes us uncomfortable, but it also keeps us free. And I believe that such men may be measured differently by our descendants. He may be our Robin Hood, our Thomas Paine, a man for our season."

"When you're right, you're right," I said. I'd been given a lesson in law by a man who never even took his cap off, but he was right and I thanked him, gave him my card just in case, and turned to leave.

"If I have to nick him again or hear anything on the wire, I'll ring up your number, sure. Good luck."

The front door was swinging closed behind me when he joined me on the street. "I'll walk a way with you, if you don't mind." I said I didn't.

"I've never met an American private detective before. This has been an exciting week here. Can you tell me if—this will sound foolish—but if you ever talk to yourself, sort of, in that interesting way, as you work—like the narrative voice in the films and novels? I like that."

I thought about it. "Yes, sometimes. I never thought about it before, but yes. I guess I learned it from the novels and movies."

He seemed to be thinking it over, too, in order to be honest. "I don't think I do. At least not often. Too bad, really. Some rather nifty metaphors in those thoughts."

"You mean like 'McNasty was the kind of guy who had the cockroaches from his building down at City Hall, demanding his eviction'?"

"Yes, yes, I like that. Wish I could do it. I talk shop with the missus. She's a bit of a crime buff. Are you talking to yourself now? It would 'make my day,' as your Dirty Harry says, to hear it."

"Harry's a philosopher I take seriously," I said. "Particularly when he says, 'A man's got to know his limitations.' But I'll try: 'I'd gotten the message that I was chasing a man everybody else wanted to protect, but I was relieved, as I rounded into Sheep Street with Inspector Talley, to see that British police inspectors still had legs and feet.' "

"That's quite good for improvisation," Talley said.

"Well, I'm no MacLeod, but I do have a license."

The radio kid came down the other side of Sheep Street. I assumed it was the same one because his head was bandaged. Talley crossed and I followed. Talley snatched the large box from the kid and turned it off.

"This is confiscated," he said. "You were warned by the judge."

"When will I get it back?" The kid was surly but scared of Talley.

"You won't. So why don't you find something else to do. Go to the library. Next time you do *this*," he said, pointing to the box, "I'll nick you proper."

The kid slouched away, kicking at the sidewalk.

"Can you make up a monologue for that?" he asked. "Something I can tell the missus."

"You do it. You can learn."

He stood in the street thinking, holding the boom box awkwardly, staring at it like a hog at a wristwatch. He cleared his throat.

"How's this? 'I had the radio. It had everything on it you could get, but they weren't playing my kind of music any more.' " He looked up like a kid for approval.

"Not bad," I said. "You're on the right track."

Officer Talley saluted me and walked back down Sheep Street with his new radio, a bounce in his step, and no doubt a little Mike Hammer in his head.

I called the Oxford don Davis said had left the message for MacLeod, and we arranged to meet the next day. He told me that a student had transcribed Jock's whole speech and would print it up. I could have asked him to mail it ahead, but that's not good detective work. If the wheels and feet don't move, the eyes don't see important details. Even Sherlock Holmes got out and walked around. I liked what they'd printed on the MacLeod-doomed program Royal Shakespeare Company play bill, from Jung:

> It is important to have a secret, a premonition of things unknown. . . . A man who has never experienced that has missed something important. He must sense that he lives in a world that is in some respects mysterious; that things happen and can be experienced which remain inexplicable; that not everything that happens can be anticipated. The unexpected and the incredible belong in this world. Only then is life whole.

I thought Talley and his missus would like that, so I asked Davis to make a copy and send it to him.

I got a call after supper from Gaunt. I asked if I should go to a pay phone.

"Not at Colonel Davis's. He's been out a while, but he keeps up with things. I talked to him a few days ago and he's had her swept, the inn. But just in case, call me at this number. We're in deeper water now."

I took it and went out to the street, passed the first booth just in case, and made the call from near the Dirty Duck. "Lay on, Macduff," I said.

A guy walking by heard me and said, "Projection!

How will they hear you in the back rows?" I flipped him the finger and he shrugged. Life in a theatrical town.

"All speculation, mind," said Bobby, "but your Scot is an electronics wizard with no head for business who went bankrupt last year. He's not heavily connected, rather an innocent, really, but he did have patents on a couple of good items and the court takes only part of that income, so he can afford to play revolutionary. If the serious lads get onto him, he'll wish he never heard the word Celt. I see him as you do. It's your old crony that interests me."

"Hold, enough," I said, really not wanting to go further, deeper.

"It's just intuition, but he could bag that money to the Provos, tuck half away for himself, give half to them for major mischief, and have bought himself some very tight security—as long as he stays handy—and a guaranteed place in the legends of his people. Songs would be sung about him, poems written. The great *sennaiche* who fooled the Roundheads and Tories on both sides of the Atlantic and kept a king's ransom for himself with no tax liability. I'd not swear to this, but a half million untaxed might be worth more than a million taxable, U.S. or U.K. If he reports it stolen, it doesn't even belong to him. Drop it into a Cayman or Swiss account. He might even be able to play it bigger, a movie. He gets to be the hero to both sides."

"He's a sot. He couldn't pull it off."

"He's got you and me running, hasn't he? You should read Miyamoto Musashi's book on strategy. He was a samurai."

"I have read it."

"Then perhaps you'll give me the pertinent passages."

"Make your enemy drunk," I said, still resisting.

"How?"

Reluctantly I acknowledged my strategy master. "By appearing to be drunk yourself."

"Just thinking. Maybe I'm wrong. I must ask you before I do this next thing. May I run a check on your Emma Poole?"

"Yes," I said, and hung up.

My phone was ringing when I got back to my room. The girl at the desk asked me to return a call to Tess, and gave me the number, and I did, Gaunt's voice still in my head.

Emma said hello. I asked her where she was. She said the Dirty Duck. I asked why she chose a noisy joint full of stage sillies. She said she thought it would be better concealment than quieter places.

"I haven't checked in. Anyway, aren't you glad I'm here, at all?"

"Sorry," I said. "Have you heard from Jock?"

"Jock? How could I have? Randy, come straight here and I'll find a thermometer and take your temperature. Are you feverish or daft? You're scarin' me."

I felt the paranoia loosen its grip a little, and I remembered that I'd already reserved a room for her under the name Tess Darbyfield—putting it on my card—at a respectable but active enough inn like the Stratford, where we wouldn't be conspicuous. Then I thought: What are *we* hiding from? Clive wouldn't mind if we made love on the RSC main stage.

"Sorry," I said. "Everything's fixed. I'll be right over."

"Be right over and what?" Emma asked.

I didn't blow this one. "Be right over and sweep you up and hold you tightly and kiss you until you swoon."

"That's better," she said. "I'll try to bum a mint or two, then, if you don't deliver the goods, report you to the police for obscene phoning."

"No good. They don't prosecute here. Besides, you'll love it."

"We'll see."

And she did see. I walked into the Dirty Duck and swept the room with raptor's eyes until I felt a golden, amber presence more than saw it, and went over and did just what I'd promised. We got a big hand from the audience, and the same guy from the street said, "Now you're *projecting!*" Although I don't wear a hat, I swept it off and bowed deeply, and Emma curtsied like a pro. When I had her in my arms I could trust her. I'd never been jealous like this before—hurt, yes, but not expecting it in advance.

As we walked outside, me holding her bags, she said, "You said at Lulworth that every time you told a woman about being a secret, dangerous sort, it came back and bit you. If that's true, can you tell me why you think it happened?"

"This may sound silly, but I think it happens when they realize that I'm not *really* dangerous, that I won't hurt them, that I can be hurt."

"That's crazy."

"My sentiments exactly. Maybe they're attracted to the abstract idea of a dangerous life and get bored when they find they can treat me like an ordinary guy. As if I were advertising falsely or something. Maybe it's about power. Sometimes I think it's *all* about power and we just call it love or security or whatever."

"What kinds of men do they leave you for?"

"That's the big puzzle. Weenies. Helpless, hopeless fuckups."

"That is a puzzle," she said. "They're crazy." She looked at me with her head cocked like a dog or a doctor. Then she shook it off and began walking briskly. "I think," she said, "that we'd better not talk about this anymore and make love as soon as possible."

"Yes, dear," I said, and followed obediently with the bags.

FIFTEEN
◆◆◆◆

THE NEXT DAY Emma went to see Clive Davis and I went to Oxford to further my education. Dr. Pembroke had left a message at Wadham to meet him for lunch at the Antiquity Hall. Perhaps, not knowing what an American detective might be like, he thought it discreet not to risk the college. As I drove to Oxford I heard a discussion on BBC-1 about Sellafield. "There are just a few of us," the environmentalist said, "but we're steady on. I wish we could have a great awakening, like Woodstock, once more."

That's only because you weren't around, pal, I thought. The Age of Aquarius lasted about ten weeks—estimates vary—and we can learn a lot from what its heroes are doing now. I'd gone a few years ago to that peninsula south of San Francisco, near La Honda and Woodside, to recover from a nasty case. I kept hearing choppers above, like Vietnam. It went on day after day. The noise was maddening, and they were stirring up dust and pollen and scaring the shit out of anything more sentient than a cow. Was it the drug wars? What was the theory, to make life on the ground so miserable the dopers would run away? I did a little detective work and learned it was Neil Young's cattle ranch chopper, looking for some fucking stray cows. I made a call. Hadn't anybody heard of horses, maybe even bush-whacking through some of those ravines on foot? I did a little commando work and left a message that got results. Woodstock. Harmonic Convergences. Quantum Leaps in Consciousness. The Global Brain Switch-on. A New World Order. Tell It to the Marines.

Antiquity Hall looked like a very grand and recent version of the English pub, with polished brass and bean sprouts and even a no-smoking section, for which I was grateful. It was at a bridge that spanned either the River Cherwell or a canal, I never learned which. I asked for the don at the desk and was let into that cherished smokeless refuge to a table where Professor Brian Pembroke sat with two almost identical students. They were both flaxen-haired youths with blue eyes. One smiled and shook my hand; the other was listening to a Walkman. He reminded me of Teddy of the Traveling Entwhistles. Pembroke was sleek and well fed as a badger in the autumn—not overweight but carrying the weight of pleasures just short of inconvenience. He had a tan. I had the impression that he put a lot of time into looking so naturally well groomed, that he was older than he looked at first. He wore a summer-weight beige suit with a paisley bow tie. In an atmosphere most often dictated by winter tweeds stained with winter and summer sweat, spotted old boy ties, bad teeth, and dandruff, Pembroke was a breath of fresh air, if slightly too sleek and subtly sinister. We exchanged pleasantries, except for the lad with the earphones. At least his music didn't leak out like the sound of some nasty electronic insect boring its way through his gray matter.

"Meet Ian, president of the union," Pembroke said, "and our young friend Dervo. He's from Bosnia-Herzegovina."

"Well, first," I said, "were you happy with Mr. MacLeod?"

The don deferred to Ian, who smiled even more broadly and said, "My God, yes. What a coup. Normally it's a chore to find a speaker, but there he was, a legend. I didn't know he was still alive."

Professor Pembroke said, after downing a sherry like a Wild West shot of red-eye, "I must confess I wasn't sure. It, or I should say he, is not within my speciality, which is Victorian. When we met, I told him I'd seen Allen Ginsberg and Gregory Corso visit here years ago, and they'd made a point of visiting our W. H. Auden, whereupon Ginsberg tried to eat Wystan's tie. He was quite appalled, which I suppose was the point."

"What did Jock say to that?" I asked Pembroke.

"He said, 'Allen is much more direct in expressing his appetites these liberated days. As for me,' he went on, 'I like living coeducational, which is to say woman, flesh—being your basic meat-and-potatoes heterosexual guy.' "

"He's a caution," I said.

"He's important, I think," Pembroke said. "Always in the front lines and yet already nearly in the canon. Having only the one book is awkward. I do hope the confusion about the other one is clarified."

"It's my impression it was stolen," I said. "Is that what you mean by confusion?"

"Yes."

"Well," said Ian. "He thinks he might get it back."

I didn't comment.

"He seems a natural rhetorician," Pembroke said. "The Irish in him, I suppose."

"I've long wondered why so many Irish poets and Scots engineers," I said.

"Calvinism, mainly," he said, "and their relative proximity to the Industrial Revolution, but yes, here are our Lake District Romantics posturing away while the Scottish ideas are becoming the Industrial Revolution just a few miles away. And the Irish writing about history like ancient bards, and even the Welsh, though they worked in the mines. I think Wordsworth grumbled about the railroads a bit, their nasty smoke."

"As did Carlyle," I offered.

"Yes, quite so. Now there's a natural rhetorician, like your MacLeod."

"He introduced us to Carlyle years ago," I said, remembering. "Said he used words like a whip, a riding crop. But there's a point at which a proper rap to the flanks becomes a beating, and if, as he felt Carlyle was in his later years, you're beating the wrong horse. . . . He was talking about slavery, and I was just mixing metaphors."

"He said as much here," Ian said. "I don't know if it's in the text of the speech I have."

"I think he was headed up Carlyle's way, to visit the grave of his former hero," I told them. We ordered. "He felt Carlyle worshiped heroes too much and didn't respect common men enough. And his support of slavery was something MacLeod couldn't forgive."

"You sound like a scholar as well as a detective," Ian said, and Pembroke made a gesture implying, ahh, the young. "He said you'd met around a university years ago. Columbia? Berkeley?"

"He talked about me?"

"Yes, the detective." When Ian said that, Dervo looked up at me, then away.

"We were at the University of South Florida," I said. "It's not as famous as the University *of* Florida, where Gatorade was invented, or Florida State, whose football coach makes half a million a year without speaking standard English, but we did have a wild bunch down there for a while, for some reason I've never discovered. No doubt Jock was the magnet."

"Tell him about that other curious topic," Pembroke said to Ian. I got my chicken curry dish and Ian and Dervo their steak and kidney pies. Pembroke had a large salad. Dervo hardly seemed to know where he was, let alone whether or not he was hungry. He poked a fork into it as a child might poke a stick into a cow patty in a field.

Ian complied: "Had he ever mentioned the datura plant to you?"

"I haven't seen the man in over twenty years," I said. "I have no idea what his interests are. Why?"

"He was at some pains to contact a biologist here. I think they even met in the morning before Mr. Mac-Leod was 'lit up' for his talk. Just curious."

"I think it's a poison and a hallucinogen, an alkaloid," I said. "It's called jimsonweed in parts of the Americas. Some Indians have used it as a psychedelic drug. I hope he's not getting into that kind of thing again. It kills cows when they eat it. Locoweed, the Hispanics call it. Any context?"

"No," Pembroke said. "Maybe the biologist is still around, although most of us are gone or packing to leave for the summer."

We ate our meal, then Ian gave me the transcript. "My number's at the top, in case you want to follow up on anything." This drew almost a scowl from the don. "I'll be here through the summer," Ian said despite the frown.

"And I'll be in Italy," Pembroke said. "Trying to locate some of Dervo's relatives, and Gore Vidal's invited us for a week."

"He's so blond," I said, of Dervo, not Vidal.

"Curious," Pembroke agreed. "I'd say a pocket of those the Romans called Circassians. Terrible mess in his homeland."

Pembroke and Ian went to the toilet, as Brits unashamedly call it. I had started to read the speech transcript when Dervo suddenly reached out and handed me an envelope. I saw my name on the front. "For you from him," he said. "Private."

"Thank you," I said. I lifted off his earphones carefully and put them on to hear what held him together. In was Chopin's Polonaise in A Flat. "Will you be all right?" I tilted my head in the direction of the men's.

He laughed. "I have two knives," he said. "I have used them before. You detective? Why people carry only one knife? One for each hand. See?"

I nodded. I did see.

SIXTEEN
◆◆◆◆

I PICKED UP the tab, which Pembroke seemed to expect, and sat in the car to read. It was a bright and breezy summer day, perfect for chasing your sweetheart's hat across a meadow of wildflowers, and how bad could it be since I had a sweetheart just a few miles away?

I realized that along with being in love and sick of MacLeod, I was homesick. I felt like calling the sisters so they could get Hayduke to bark for me. I almost did, since I needed to check in anyway, but the time difference meant waking them, so I faced the music.

First the letter:

> Dear Gato,
>
> After all these years, it's a pleasure to say hello. I have some serious business here. You never took me seriously after your commando routine. I was just Prankstering. Well, pranks may save the world. I can't say how I know that, and I admit I have some personal problems, so I'm counting on you for the traditional American cliff-hanger rescue. I am, after all, working with chaos—first expanding

it, then substituting. I'm lately interested in the datura plant, one of the few we didn't try. You remember opening that package of peyote buds mailed from Joe's Cactus Ranch, Laredo, Texas. Projectile vomiting, then hallucinations for at least twelve hours. Those were the days.

Man at the university here thinks datura is an ingredient in zombie powder, but he also says it *eats* plutonium! Imagine a plant that can be both enlightening and at least a symbolic threat to the nuclear nabobs. I haven't gone beyond that, and maybe I'm just trying to be Merlin when I really ought to be in rehab, but I tell you this: The road leads north. I go to prepare a place for you. If it were not so, I would have told you. God, I hope I guessed right and they sent you and not some merciless Pinkerton.

Well, I'm prepared for anything. My forefathers include the clan patriarch Fierce Wolf *Liotr*, from the Norwegian *Ljot Ulfr*. Consider me your spiritual guide to a new world. Like Kazantzakis's or even Tennyson's version of Ulysses, I'm cursing the gods and heading for the pole, the icy end of the world—him south, me north. These poles may melt if the Busyness as Usual Crowd stay in power, and places like England and our beloved Florida will be underwater. Well, Florida's already flooded with assholes from Ohio, but this Britain is a finisher. Whatever I seek, I'll find it in the north. Trust me. Couldn't you just eat Emma like a beef and kidney pie? No trifle she, but a woman to stick to your ribs. See you in the future.

Your old friend,

James MacLeod, son of Fierce Wolf Liotr.

I read his address to the Oxford Union.

"Dear fellow decadent spoiled brats, you are not stardust, nor are you golden, to disabuse us of any Aquarian nostalgia. Your chief contribution, in my view, has been to frighten yourselves so with the fury of your debauchery that some of you, like Thomas Merton, who was at Columbia like me, Kerouac, Ginsberg, et al., or like your wonderful Ved Mehta, who prepped at the Arkansas School for the Blind, are forced to seek God. Others, like me, continue in decadence, hoping God will find us. We wait like accidents on highways. Surely someone will call the Supreme Ambulance. (Laughter) So is it clearly understood that I condemn myself with you? Good. The world needs no more sweet, well-intentioned folk. It chews them up and spits them back into our streets at an industrial rate, and they sleep under cardboard or work as drones in hospitals, welfare offices, schools. The world needs what we know, which is how bad things can be, how low human motives can sink.

"Let me compare us with the datura plant, which one of your biologists told me only this morning has the ability to consume plutonium, engorge it, take its poison into itself and survive—nay, thrive. How remarkable and, at present, how useless. But let us continue with this metaphor. This plant, cousin to the lowly but wholesome potato and also known as jimsonweed, locoweed, and thorn apple, produces fruit which, along with its leaves, either kills animals like us or, if carefully prepared, opens new channels of power, real power, mind and spirit power. Call it the anarchic power of the Weed. What are we to the workaday potato world? Not exotic hothouse flowers, I suggest, but Weeds!

"We live in a world that has adjusted, God help us, to plutonium and all its deadly propensities, but not to datura. We easily understand the economic reasons for this—though how we arrived at this economic dependence is fully as hallucinatory as the specters of any drug-besotted Indian or raver or whatever you're calling your hippies these days—which, by the way, are a slander upon true hippies. *(Laughter here)*

"What if that world were thrown out of adjustment by some phenomenon like the datura plant? What if it has been in the shadow of disapproval or ignorance for this very opportunity? If there is a Creator, what if this is the purpose—given certain kinks in history—for this odd and disreputable creation? Mind you, this is all metaphor.

"I'm not suggesting that you use datura or plant it near nuclear *plants. (More laughter at the pun)* See what I'm getting at? I'm saying simply consider the datura into the scheme of things. Juxtapose our insane reliance on radioactive ores against this new natural enemy of theirs, this new predator, as it were. What, still metaphorically, could it possibly be but the very antithesis of the so-called logic and science that led us into a situation in which by splitting the atom, we have invented a new kind of poison, a poison we don't know how to get rid of? I note in passing that you have a nuclear reclamation plant on the coast of the Irish Sea. (*Boo, anger*)

"While I disavow much of what Carlyle thought and wrote in his late, angry years—his misanthropy and racism—I know what he'd have said about that. He'd have said, 'Quack.' Yes, sheer quackery, the rattle of what seems to be logic and of the great, ugly, industrial machine that Carlyle so despised, and seated in the locomotive are the quacks who explain the wonder and use of it all. If that be logic, then some new or antilogic must be found. If plutonium is a dangerous by-product and the stramonium substance for which *Datura stramonium* is named is also dangerous, but *its* plant will eat plutonium, the indestructible wonder element, then perhaps we have a useful metaphorical battle: stramonium versus plutonium.

"Think of the fear the threat of widespread stramonium use would cause. Then think of simply using that fear to open the debate. If you're afraid of our plant, then aren't we justified in being afraid of yours? Perhaps neither has a useful place in our world, and both should be made as little of as possible. Let each danger be canceled out by reminding us of the other. Datura has spread all over the tropical and temperate world. So, now, has nuclear power. While plutonium and nuclear energy are modern, datura is ancient. Perhaps it is useful to see it as a natural, metaphorical counterforce. Do with it what you will.

"These are unpolished ideas, but I believe they fall, like datura seed, on ground which, though it may be ancient and leached of nutrients, can support a good, mischievous weed seed. I'm heading north. There may be some bloom of ambivalent energy this season; there may not. Keep your eyes and ears open for some event in which dark forces may be considered, laid open to frighten the world to its senses. Magic is risky. It's too much for your sweet-minded reformer. It can turn bloody at any moment, or worse than bloody. It needs cultivation by other weeds like us, those unafraid of damnation and hellfire, those who'll take risks that when the power is theirs, their hearts will recover the good that's in us all—not the easy virtue of the un-tempted, the simpleton, but the hard-won, fire-tempered steel of those who'll risk singeing and reach into the flame. I think this is the right audience for this message.

"I'm researching my own Scots roots—thorn apple, most likely (Much laughter)—and in so doing I found a quote from George Buchanan, Scots historian, who said, when warned that the king might not approve his thoughts: 'If I have told the truth, I will bide his feud and all his kin's then.' A last reminder: Primitive as their motives were and simple as their desires, our ancient ones knew both how to drink and eat, and vomit for the dogs, and fall asleep upon the rushes or on stone or earthen floors, and how to get up the next day and fight. Those who didn't perished with the unfittest. Rediscover the knighthood in you. Relearn the battle lust. There are dragons out there. (Loud applause)

"Just a few words about another so-called progressive idea much in vogue these days. Sometimes it's called bio-regionalism, other times, local or self-rule. I try to believe that the sincere liberals and radicals who promote it are not so ideological that they refuse to see the consequences—most terribly in what was until recently the Soviet bloc. I grew up in a climate that encouraged us to think of ourselves as all one people, our cultural and racial difference only interesting variations, nothing to fight about. I still believe it.

"Later I came to believe that our main enemy was the corporate consumerist capitalism of my own country and others—the Huxley nightmare, which did, as I predicted, outlast the Orwellian. I still believe that. And to fight a monolithic power base like corporations, we need the power of unity, a world democracy that will decide for people and not exploitative Frankensteinian monsters Adam Smith never dreamed of. This idea of world government got no further than the cold war, in which we called the Huxleyian nightmare the first world, the Orwellian the second, and the third world perhaps could be named for Jonathan Swift, who had a modest proposal for both hunger and overpopulation. (*Laughter*)

"With the fall of the Iron Curtain, we've seen a lot of good and bad results, but the one intolerable result is the degeneration of what were, granted, totalitarian monoliths like the U.S.S.R. and Yugoslavia into vicious tiny groups no larger in many cases than the nasty little clans from which my people came. This strikes me as nothing less than a catastrophic breakdown of centuries of civilization.

"Listen to me. This is unpopular, but I know it to be true. Do not dignify this balkanization or local autonomy or cultural/regional autonomy or state's rights or whatever else it's called any more than you would approve the return of the Mongol horde or the Roman Empire. Do recognize that some worldwide management of these clans is absolutely necessary if we are not to end up in the second—or for all we know, the third or fourth—Dark Ages. If we don't do it through some organization like the U.N., the fucking corporations will, and they have no thought for the future, for the human spirit, for anything beyond the bottom line for next quarter. They will sell us until we're too poor and sick and stupid to afford their products. Then, like earlier barbarian kings, they will disappear, leaving only the trace of their pollution or perhaps the utter destruction of our world. If any survive, we will savage one another from our tiny enclaves until there is no human life left to destroy.

"How is it possible that we must now divide Croats from Serbs; Bosnians from Herzegovinians; and, as one grim pundit put it, Sloves from -enians? *(Laughter)* If the Poles and Italians and African Americans and Jews can live together in Chicago, by God, so can you. And if you can't, dammit, don't tear the hearts from your people and expect others to come to your rescue over petty grievances.

"Listen! If you are an Armenian living in a tiny enclave inside Azerbaijan, pack up and, with all due respect, get your ass out of that country to Armenia, where the majority of your people live, instead of fighting a stupid and futile war to impose your will on the majority where you live. Everybody has to move now and then. You'll be passing, I hope, Azerbaijanis from Armenia going the other way. You can swap houses. Seriously, this is already being done.

"I say this as a person seeking his own ethnic and cultural roots. It isn't that important. We're all mongrels and wanderers. The very word Scot means 'wanderer' in Irish, and it turns out most of my kin were raider Vikings from Norway. Our cultures are interesting, but you won't preserve them by fighting wars or trying to get all the documents and road signs in your new home printed in your old language instead of learning the fucking new one. Play the bagpipes, do the polka, wear veils, or go naked in your own places, but stop trying to impose your will or your self-pity on others. I'm angry. Anybody notice? We should all be angry at having to witness this nonsense. If you're a Catholic living in Northern Ireland, start walking south. You'll find a mainly Catholic Irish Free State. And if the Scots-Irish there like Protestant neighbors so much, they can bloody fucking well move back to Scotland. There's a lot of open land up north."

"What about your own Scottish nationalist views we've heard about?" a student asked.

"I'm rethinking that," said MacLeod. "Travel is broadening. A foolish consistency is the hobgoblin of little minds. At a time when the world could be making itself decent, we are acting in the age-old way that called forth dictators. If we don't get it right fast, either Orwell's or Huxley's or some new hell will be soon upon us. Today I've recommended both anarchy and a New World Order. With Whitman I say, I contradict myself? Very well, I contradict myself. I am great. I contain multitudes. With Carlyle I say, 'Be no longer a chaos, but a world, or worldkin.' Isn't *worldkin* a good word for a good world? Again, and finally, I say: Relearn the battle lust, but be sure your cause is just.

"I did not intend for that to rhyme. I leave that to Jesse Jackson. *(Laughter)* Anyway, thank you for your attention. I understand the custom now is to read something instructive or amusing and get drunk. As usual, I have forged ahead on my own." *(Applause, loud and prolonged)*

I sat in the car for a long time. I think amazement is the word. Then I drove back to Stratford-on-Avon, where I hoped my true love waited.

SEVENTEEN
◆◆◆◆

EXCEPT SHE WAS working the bar until eleven. I washed
up and had supper and walked around, then went in
and pretended not to know her while we had small talk.
Colonel Davis even came along and tried to introduce
us, but he couldn't keep a straight face, and we all
laughed. "Emma has a staff room at the back," he said.
"I think she's splendid. You do understand my rule
about fraternization?"

He got me. My jaw dropped. Then I heard Emma
laughing and Davis's face formed a big grin. "You really
have a lot of fun, don't you?" I said.

"The best of everything," he said, rubbing his head.
"If I only had your hair and your age and your girlfriend. *Then* I would have everything."

It was a good way to end the day. Emma asked if
anything good had come from the trip to Oxford, and
I said nothing. I would never let her see that speech.
Jock had reached out from wherever he was and put a
shadow on me again. He was too much, and he just
never quit, and somehow he seemed to be getting better. He had to crash sometime, but could I last?

We went to my room after she got off, or I should say

she came later at a discreet interval. I knew it wouldn't take much and somebody'd say that the Stratford was supplying call girls, but I'd be on the road tomorrow, though I hadn't decided where.

We'd just come close when the phone rang. It was Gaunt. "What do you know about the datura plant?" he asked.

What? "More than I care to know, and I'm just in bed after a long day, and I don't want to go to a pay phone or even think about that word you used."

He laughed. It surprised me. "Getting to be a bit of a Hobbit in our old age, are we? Not interested in eating any nails or glass, either, I suppose."

I laughed a little. "Yes, just me crackers and milk, a chapter of Dickens, and sweet dreams." Emma kicked me under the covers.

"Even Hobbits go on dangerous quests. How about we meet tomorrow? Urgent, or at least stuff of immediate interest. The Green Man Inn, in Saffron Walden. Take the M11 south of Cambridge, take the B road cutoff at Wendens Ambo, then follow the signs on another B road to Saffron Walden. You'll see the Green Man before you get to the town. He's—"

"I know what the Green Man is," I said. "Nature's avenger, Dionysus, Bacchus, Robin Hood, maybe the Jolly Green Giant."

"I thought you might," Bobby said. "That's what this is all about. When's convenient?"

"Threeish?"

"Make it two. We may have a lot to do."

Emma and I had a lot to do, but it was refreshing, restorative, restful.

* * *

The Green Man was remodeled from an older, smaller inn. One of his many images was on the pub sign. Actually, if you didn't know his history, you could miss the shape of a man's shoulders and head growing out of leaves, in this case with leaves growing out of his mouth and ears. I looked at the cars, usually a clue to what's inside. There were family minivans, compacts—suggesting a traveling and local clientele, which is to say normal. There were also utility vans; motorcycles, on- and off-road; and more four-wheel-drive vehicles than I'd ever seen at once in England. I wondered how they mixed.

Although there was a wood carving of Greenie running the length above the bar mirror, there was no other reference, and the folks finishing late lunches or early pints didn't look like medievalists or whatever sort of rough beast Gaunt's crew might be to have adopted the ancient figure.

Greenie had been adopted many times. He was a pagan tree spirit in many forms, probably an important part of Druidic worship; he'd been Dionysus and Bacchus; he was probably the model for Robin Hood, the epitome of creative anarchy against evil; the stonemasons who built churches carved him into many a chapel and cathedral, often undetected by the churchmen below. He was the spirit of nature, teaching us to be more natural and sometimes punishing us for neglecting or harming Mother Earth.

That was why he'd been embraced recently by environmentalists, especially those of the radical persuasion. He stood for that in nature which would stand for no more. He had slept for centuries, but now he was awake and very angry. This was the hypothesis of some New Agers.

I saw Gaunt in the mirror and spun my stool, just to show him he couldn't creepy-crawl me, that I was still on my toes. It would have been more impressive if it hadn't been a stationary bar chair, which I nearly broke.

Many British pubs lack bar mirrors. Was it because they were older and custom then did not value mirrors for drinkers, or were they universal in the United States because we *needed* to see who was coming up behind us?

"Lads are waiting for you in the back," he said. I followed.

It was two pubs: one for the ordinaries in the front and one in back for the Merry Men. We passed a door that was marked PRIVATE, walked past the women's and men's toilets, turned a corner, and followed the hall to a rear entrance to the kitchen. A woman cutting luncheon meat on a machine slicer nodded at Bobby. We walked to the freezer door and then inside. He turned on a light switch and closed the door behind us.

"Cool," I said.

"Very funny," he said.

"Why not use the private door?"

"It's steel and heavily reinforced. It can be opened for inspectors and the like as a private dining room for clubs and such, but we come in this way." He pulled down on a meat hook and a narrow door in the back wall of the freezer swung open into a large room. We walked through and Bobby pushed a switch on what appeared to be a light fixture and we watched the door close until we heard its locking mechanism catch. There was a mist of frost momentarily in the air.

"Looks cold out," one of the men said from the long

bar. "It was summer when I come in here. I've missed me supper."

There was general laughter while Gaunt grinned at me like Puck and I grinned back, probably like Huck in Tom Sawyer's gang's cave.

There was no smoke. In fact, every convention of the English pub was altered just slightly so that for me it *was* a kind of Midsummer Night's Dream. "We go out the way we came in, but a few at a time," Bobby said, "except for emergencies. For that we use one or two or both quick exits that you ain't cleared to know about yet."

"How's the owner feel about this?"

"I like it fine," Gaunt said.

"Ah, risky venture? Call a risk junkie."

"This is a harmless game. It'll be packed up and turned into what it pretends to be within the month."

"Why?"

"We're about to take some real risks," Gaunt said. "Split up, go underground, operate as cells, ad hoc squads. This is our last recruitment."

One of his mates said, "Curious bugger, ain't he, boss? He already knows more than a bleedin' first-year Mason."

There was a sign, one of many above the bar, that read: WARNING: IF WE GET DRUNK AND REVEAL CLASSIFIED INFORMATION, WE'RE UNDER ORDERS TO KILL ONE AN-OTHER. I took it to be a spoof of special ops hot-dog talk. There was an enlarged photo of a group of men who'd pulled down their camo trousers so that only their asses could be seen. The caption read: FROM ALL THE GANG AT THE BELTON BAR IN MONTANA, A GREAT BIG HOWDY, AND FUCK ALL YOU LIMEY BLOKES. WE'D SHOW

OUR FACES, BUT WE'VE GOT SECURITY CONCERNS AND BE-
SIDES, THEY'RE NOT AS GOOD LOOKING. RESIST MUCH,
OBEY LITTLE. KEEP 'EM BUSY ON THAT SIDE. There was
another enlarged photo of a billboard that said: BILL-
BOARDS ARE A DAILY INSULT TO THE INTELLIGENCE OF
AUSTRALIANS AS WELL AS HUMANS. COURTESY BUGAUP.
Flames were rising from below almost to the point of
consuming the message. There was an enlarged photo
of Dr. Paul Watson's new environmental fighting ship,
the *Sea Shepherd*. The first one had been attacked and
disabled by Navy SEALs. Everywhere a different image
of the Green Man, including a mural of some skill
showing him dispatching a whaling ship. There were
mounted heads on the walls: Reagan, Thatcher, Bush,
Quayle, James Watt, others.

I took the bar to be something I liked very much,
something I'd already made contact with in the States,
but wouldn't have expected here. But why not? The
Brits were, if anything, more respectful of nature, having experienced all the ills of the Industrial Revolution
on this small island and still kept it green. And since
they had given us our tradition of the common man
turning his skill at arms from the enemies of his government to the enemy that was his government, why
shouldn't they be walking point on the environmental
battlefield? I'd known Vietnam vets in the states who'd
done a little demolition on behalf of Mother Earth,
using the skills they were taught in jungles and forests
they came to love almost as much as those at home. Ed
Abbey wrote about it until he died, and Doug Peacock,
his model for arch-monkey-wrencher George Hayduke,
was the closest thing we had to a living, angry Green

Man. Now, it seemed, I was in a pub full of them. I took them to be operators as skilled as Gaunt who had worked and were now working against the whalers, oilers, nukes, and the rest of what Carlyle called "The Aristocracy of the Moneybag."

"I want you to meet Randall Gatsby Sierra," Gaunt said. Our entrance had been so sudden that there was no time for small talk, and I hadn't even gotten a good look at him after all these years. His hair was still short and dark auburn, with a slight fading at the temples, and his neck above the T-shirt collar was lined like the bottom of a dry wash out in Abbey's canyon country. He was fit, as I expected. Only recently retired, he'd been one of Salman Rushdie's bodyguards. He had the perfect paratrooper's body, maybe the perfect fighter's body. He was a middleweight now, probably at 170, with the reach and punching power of a heavyweight. He had large, strong hands, as I remembered from when we partnered up for unarmed combat. His ears were close to his head and his profile was Roman, hawklike, his nose the only obvious target. There was little of Gaunt to hit and a lot of him to hit you. He looked exactly like his name.

I saw the same intensity in his movements and posture. People like Bobby always seemed to be working at something challenging, and I suppose I did, too, even with my middle-aged Hobbit habits. Now Bobby's direction was one he really seemed to believe in.

"I'll stand for Randy anywhere," he said to the group. "If he's willing, I propose him for membership." He looked at me, serious.

"Membership in what?"

"You've looked around," he said. "You tell us what. That's the first part of initiation anyway. If you decide you don't like it, you must keep this in confidence. Agree to that?"

"Yes, if you assure me that innocent people don't suffer."

"I'll tell you that they don't suffer directly. We don't blow up hotels and put bombs in baby prams. I'll start the questioning. Who's the enemy?"

Hell, this was easy, my hobbyhorse just as Shakespeare was Davis's, but how did he know? "Those who don't recognize that consumer, corporate capitalism is consuming the earth. We can't keep growing our way out of every economic problem."

"Why not?" asked a bearded guy at a nearby table.

"Because it merely puts off the responsibility, and because as long as we do it, we can never afford to face the main problem, which is too many people."

"But they say Malthus was wrong because we have new agronomy, super plants, fertilizers." It was the same guy.

"Malthus never got around to the spiritual economy," I said. "What's the point of feeding billions of people if all they're good for is to consume and live like rats in cages?"

Heads nodded. I felt a little like MacLeod.

"We need a stable-state economy," I said, "but that's not acceptable to corporations, who want more than healthy businesses that offer goods and services and employ workers. They want to squeeze out every dime, and that means exploitation, which the earth can no longer sustain."

"Say more about spiritual impact," said a guy at the bar. Nobody laughed. He was wearing a hard hat.

"This system turns us into desperate little bill-paying conformists who can only temporarily be amused by empty promises and new gadgets."

"What's to be done?" A tall guy dressed all in black—Irish, maybe.

"Monkey wrench. Shoes in the machinery. Keep 'em guessing and keep 'em on the run. Keep their worst offenses in the media and undercut their profits with sabotage, psywar, pranks. Teach the public to laugh at them."

"Why do we do this and not others? What about the courts et cetera?" The guy with the beard again.

"We do it because we can, and the courts are too slow and too often owned by the rich. Because we're privileged to know how. Let the other well-meaning folks do it in court, agencies, public office, the pulpit. We do it in the dark or suddenly in daylight because we can."

"Isn't that terrorism?" A guy in overalls.

"Yes. Terror might do these fuckers some good. Their main fear is being poor, powerless."

"Then why not kidnap them, even kill executives?" Same guy.

"Because it's too risky. The Exxon exec was kidnapped for ransom but died of a heart attack before he could be released. We haven't come close to exhausting our other tactics, which the public can enjoy. If we keep a sense of humor and try to love even the assholes we're trying to stop, we can cultivate public goodwill, let them know there's something that does not love a wall.

Blow the shit out of their property, if it's not hazardous to others, but if we take up human terrorism, we'll bring maximum heat on ourselves and lose our support—unspoken though it may be—and lose the battle, because we'll have lost our own integrity—like the IRA, for example."

The guy in black again. "I was in the IRA. I agree, but what about the single mother who works for, say, Sellafield? It's the best job she ever had, and her kids can go to good schools. Along come you and somehow get the plant shut down. And there she is on the dole."

"Are you serious?" I asked. "This is a tragedy? Better to be on the dole than glow in the dark. Give her help getting a better job. Until these fat asses *get* shut down, nobody will develop safe energy. There may be alternatives, but there's no way to keep everyone happy and still change the world. She needs to know more than she wants to know about what's under that building. Don't tell me she isn't scared. What was her last radiation reading? How many roentgens has she absorbed today of 'harmless' radioactivity? Is the leukemia figure just a coincidence in that part of Britain? Trying to keep everybody happy is what *got* us into this mess. Ask yourselves what happens to the loggers when the trees are all cut down? Will the company take care of them? Fuck keeping everybody happy. Keep everybody as scared as they should be."

"I've heard enough," said the man in overalls. "He's far too radical. I say we turn him over to the coppers."

After a pause, everybody laughed. "Give the man a drink," said the man in black. "I'll try and get him in the IRA."

"Don't forget the IRA are trying to get you into a

body bag, Falcon," Gaunt said. "Anyway, he doesn't drink."

"That's it," said the whole bar in a theatrical babble. "Out with him. He's not one of us."

"You passed the first part," Gaunt said.

"Have you been indoctrinating Jock MacLeod?" I asked. "Did he get all that datura shit from you?"

"Swear to God, no. That's why I called. Some of our lads heard his speech and we thought maybe you and him was up to some Greenie capers, and we figured we'd better get our watches synchronized."

"There goes my explanation," I said. "There goes logic."

"You must know there's not a lot of logic to this," Gaunt said. "Some of it's downright mysterious, supernatural even. I think our Green Man really is among us."

"What made you think I'd be a candidate?"

"A phone call to the States," Gaunt said.

I drank a soda as Bobby introduced me up and down the bar, nicknames only. Mine was to be Kung Fu for no reason I could grasp. Bobby didn't pick, but that was what the first man called me and the rest followed, and there it was. "I'd rather fancied Dances with Wolves," I said.

"That's my name," said the man in overalls.

Nobody had mentioned the second part.

I was getting my usual afternoon fade, so I got a pot of tea. "Put some honey in it," Bobby told the barman. "And while you're at it, a double whiskey for me. Bushmill's." Gaunt almost never drank.

When we'd small-talked our way through the teapot and his whiskey, Bobby checked his watch. "By the time we get there, those as have jobs will be off. Happy hour. Sound right, mates?"

They cheered. I asked, "What, where, who?"

"This is a secret initiation," Bobby said. "It won't be much of a secret if I tell you, now will it?"

EIGHTEEN
◆◆◆◆

WE LEFT THROUGH the freezer. I reminded Bobby that he hadn't shown me the emergency exits. "You're not in yet," he said, and walked ahead of me through the other Green Man with a smugness that made me want to slap his head.

"You're really getting a kick out of this," I said.

"You'll understand when it's over why I'm telling you that this next part will hurt me as much as it does you. Did your old man ever tell you that before he smacked your bum?"

"Yes, but you ain't him," I said in my best Michael Caine.

"And I won't be the one smackin' your bum, either," he said, and we walked across the parking lot to his Land Rover and headed south on the M11. I watched the compass swing around to south-southwest and rode quietly.

I didn't pay much attention to where we got off, and it occurred to me that I'd been lax. I might have to beat it out of wherever Gaunt was taking us. I reckoned we were in the industrial suburbs, maybe London's East End, when he found a parking place. We locked up and

I followed him down the street and around the corner to a pub named the Black Watch. I remembered that was the name of the Scottish mercenary outfit that fought for the British.

We walked inside and waited for our eyes to adjust as the doors closed behind us. Lots of smoke here, parachutes hanging from the ceiling. At the far corner of the bar were replicas of road signs pointing to Lucy's Tiger's Den, Bangkok, and Don Quixote, la Cantina de los Mercenarios, in Guatemala City. Another sign proclaimed FLY AIR AMERICA and still another read: MEET INTERESTING PEOPLE AND KILL THEM. I figured we were at the major British merc bar. How many of these were real and how many were wanna-bes I didn't know, but I still wasn't sure it was important.

"Oh, shit," said a voice I couldn't trace. "Not again. It's the little green men, the tree fairies." There was a dramatic hush, during which about ten men left.

"I have the honor to announce," Gaunt said in his sergeant's voice, "that this bar is full of sodden geezers who couldn't put a bullet anywhere with accuracy unless it might be up an Arab boy's arse during foreplay. You know the drill. I count some twenty heads here, most of them empty. The usual formality is for me to remind you that you are bouncers in life's whorehouse, which keeps you in touch with your mums. I could and will add insults if required. Otherwise, let us proceed directly to a fight between the Green Man sponsor, which I am, and our initiate, whose name is none of your business. The fight is conducted at force level seven, which means that things may be broken but not removed or permanently disfigured. The odds this evening are about ten to one, which, I'm afraid, gives us the edge. I think that just about covers it, except that on this special occasion my friend and I will sing a song I taught him when we were training to be what we are now, the most formidable fighters the world has ever seen. Perhaps this song can become part of the tradition of our ceremony, if your livers hold up, those of you who survive today. The song is called, appropriately, "I Don't Want to Join the Navy." Remember it, Kung Fu? This key all right? Hmmmm."

I tried to hum and see if I could even make a noise beyond humming. I wasn't sure it could be heard beyond, but a certain dry and choked sound did issue forth.

"Remember the other slogan?" he asked me quietly. "What do you do when disarmed, vastly outnumbered, and surrounded by the enemy?"

"Kill them, sir," I said tentatively.

"I can't *hear* you," he said.

"Kill them, sir!" I managed. I had my voice back. These might be my last words.

Gaunt led, but I remembered and joined in. It reminded me of Sean Connery and Michael Caine in *The Man Who Would Be King*, except our song was lewd.

> "I don't want to join the Navy.
> I don't want to go to sea.
> I just want to hang around
> Picadilly Underground,
> Livin' off the likes of the
> High-class ladies.
> Monday I touched her on the ankle.
> Tuesday I touched her on the knee.

Wednesday with much success
I lifted up her dress.
Thursday it was plain to see.
Friday I put me hand upon it.
Saturday she gave me balls a tweak.
But it was Sunday after supper
When I rammed the old boy up her,
And now she's gainin' thirty quid a week.
Oh Lordy . . .
I don't want a bullet up me arsehole.
I don't want me buttocks shot away.
I just want to stay in England,
Stay in merry, merry England,
And fornicate me bloomin' life away."

Then the fight began. There are theories and strategies about unarmed combat with bad odds. The Army has a good six-month school. Musashi wrote about it. There's a karate kata called Kansaku that rehearses for such a scenario—one against many. I'd thought about it now and then and had some general principles:

1. Attack where you're not expected. Slip the closest guy and take out somebody who's not expecting you, a surprise target. (This also confuses opponents who do not expect you to move so.)

2. Keep moving. Don't take a stand and try to outhack them. Half your game is running and letting them run into one another. So we tried to know where the other was, but Gaunt and I didn't stand back to back and slug it out.

3. *Take* him out. One technique per customer, if possible, but finish him. You don't want to have to fight him again.

4. Use the location. Aikido is good with misdirection of the opponent and Aikijutsu goes further to suggest that he be misdirected into bar stools, tables, aquariums, etc., as you break his limbs and joints while so directing.

But when it happens, all theory is, unless it's been internalized, useless. You go on automatic. We did, and it went on for a good while. Five minutes is a very long time to fight. Ours went maybe seven. We didn't win; we didn't lose. It became a standoff. Those still standing faced us, and we seemed to be upright, too. It seemed to everyone an honorable conclusion. My left arm was numb from a blow to the elbow, and my right was too exhausted to raise. I couldn't see from my right eye, but that was my worst one anyway. My knees? I moved them; they wobbled like rubber as usual, but they had held! Gaunt should have warned me so I could have gotten braces.

He was bleeding heavily from a scalp wound, and I suspect someone had gone beyond the rules, but then they were never very clear anyway. I think we'd put maybe ten of them in the way of hospital care. The bartender gave Gaunt a reasonably clean towel for his scalp and returned my glasses, which I'd tossed to him instinctively, and we were able to walk out and drive north with honor.

It was strange walking through the normal Green Man and into the kitchen, me with a swollen red eye and him with his head in a dirty turban that was by now red. By the time we'd passed through the freezer, I felt very good. Adrenaline burned off, endorphin count way up. We stepped out into a room of warm applause. Gaunt sat down and the tall guy in black brought a bottle of vodka and a first-aid kit to clean up and stitch his scalp.

"Don't tell me that wasn't heaven, Sierra," Gaunt said, more animated than I'd ever seen him. "It makes no sense to fight or go to war, but, by jumping Jesus God Almighty, it feels good after."

"Yes, sir!" was all the answer I could think of.

"You made officer rank," he said. "Don't 'sir' me."

"A sergeant major, as you well know, is worth ten thousand lieutenants," I said, "and you may be one of the few of any rank who can stop me from calling you sir."

I heard a high-pitched, ululating sound that passed through the whole crew and grew in volume. Then it came in discernible howls. They were howling like wolves, like Hayduke. I joined in, and it felt very good. I don't know what the Green Man thought, but I knew what Emma would think, and as soon as I got back to Stratford, I got to know how she felt—first angry at the risk, then protective and nurselike, then loving me wildly, taking some of the battle lust from me. It hurt like hell even though she tried to be careful, but I didn't complain.

NINETEEN
◆◆◆◆

THE NEXT DAY I drove north for the Lake District, with reservations at a hotel called Highfield, where MacLeod stayed. It was in Keswick (pronounced "Kessick") on Derwent Water, which was both a river and, in this location, a lake. People didn't make the distinctions about the shapes of Derwent Water unless it was absolutely necessary; it was water and it was called Derwent. Nearby were the cottage and surrounding high fields and lakes where Wordsworth, Coleridge, and some of the other Romantics found their natural inspiration. Coleridge supplemented his natural inspiration with laudanum—alcohol with opium. I'd heard a story in grad school about Coleridge, loaded on the lovely stuff, writing "Kubla Khan," when he was interrupted by "a person from Porlock on business" and lost the rest of the inspiration and the poem. As a Floridian I knew that he'd traveled there and seen the fabulous springs, his model for "Alph the sacred river." As a Cuban American, I knew that in Batista's days, Mr. Du Pont, who owned plastics and chemicals and Delaware, built what he called his "pleasure dome" in Varadero, Cuba, to "entertain" his guests. I'm sure he had sufficient security to keep any "person from Porlock" from interrupting his inspiration.

It was overcast and rained fitfully until about the time I reached the Lake District, so when the sun came out, it gave me its best, a clean polish on every leaf and stone.

The Sellafield protests and the hippie push toward Stonehenge had been on the radio, both stories refusing to go away, building momentum. Of course, all it would take to kill the Sellafield story would be a few more days with no results or a hot new story or scandal, and the hippies were old news once the solstice had come and gone with the police cordon holding.

Highfield was as pleasant in its way as the Rising Sun and much roomier, with a view of the lake and handy access to both Keswick and the shrines to the Romantics. I'd driven a long way that day, so I had supper, took a walk along the lake, and went to my room. It was late enough to check in with the sisters as they began tomorrow morning back on Puget Sound. No news. Hayduke missed me. I told Mary Katherine about Father/Brother Michael and his video and she said she'd have a look. "We're looking for production values as well as inspiration," she said. "We don't want to beam up amateur video." I told her she sounded like God's agent, and she laughed and said God was with William Morris.

I took a shower and caught the Lowatollah on the soundless TV as I was toweling off. He wore the same white Druidlike robe and a somewhat different variety of gold and silver chains with pendants—one an ankh and the other a silver and turquoise concho belt buckle like the ones the Navajos make. I turned up the sound to hear his version of what Carlyle called "transcendental moonshine." When a reporter asked him if he weren't just a rebel without a cause, he said, "Absolutely not. My causes are individualism, pantheism, Wessex regionalism within the concept of a United Regions of Europe, and polygamy and polyandry within a polymorphous society." Well, maybe he did have a program, but he still looked like Dr. Cohen, my dentist.

If this was the charismatic leader, it was easy to understand why these kids were standing around in the mud looking like road warriors who'd forgotten how to make war and were of gas anyway, so what the hell. The reporters talked with a few of the hippies on the site, some in their thirties and forties. There were young ravers who liked to take large doses of drugs and dance ecstatically to nasty, ear-damaging disco music. There were leftover punkers and blond "rude boys" with bleached dreadlocks. There were lost souls of all ages who had vaguely nontraditional lifestyles and seemed just along for the ride until they had to go back to work. And there were earnest New Age nomads, who seemed something like the hippies from now ancient history for whom they were named. It would take more than the Lowatollah to galvanize this tribe of lost souls. Somebody like MacLeod? God, don't let that happen. This was too weird already, with Gaunt and MacLeod both interested in datura and possibly in each other. To what purpose?

The tribes had a dialect of their own. They would blag a roll-up, which could be tobacco or cannabis, or they could blag a fellow camper to go back to college and become a veterinarian. Apparently *blag* meant persuade or convince or even con out of.

I got some ice for my eye and worked my arm, which was no longer numb but made me wish it was. Somebody had hit my funny bone hard, but somebody had also nearly dislocated the shoulder. I found abrasions and bruises I hadn't seen before. A fingernail was broken far back into the quick and was still bleeding. Not only was my eye swollen but now the white was completely red. My right ear was torn at the top. Somebody had tried to pull it down and off. I had a broken toe and a sprained finger. Pain prioritizes: You don't feel the smaller ones until the large ones are soothed. Thinking of pain to come and ranking that potential, I wondered if The Biggest Hurt would come from the Pict, the Scot, MacLeod, Gaunt, Emma, or somebody I had yet to meet, like these road people I was watching on TV.

I finally gave up on patching myself and went down to ask the desk for some first aid. The owners or managers were Mr. and Mrs. Farley, both of whom had almost orange hair. They looked so much alike that I wondered if they were brother and sister. Actually, they'd simply introduced themselves, not as husband and wife. I didn't care anyway, I was hurting so much. I told them I'd been mugged in London.

The next morning I had an English killer breakfast—post-fight replenishment of blood and flesh. I was almost clear of the dining room when someone's newspaper caught my eye. The man had finished and folded, so I asked if I could have a quick look at the back page of the section he'd just read. One small headline read: LOCAL FARMER BLAMES THORN APPLE FOR SHEEP BREAK-

OUT. I didn't know if the sheep had broken out or suffered an outbreak of something. An enterprising lay-out person had seen the relation and run near it a science story: BIOLOGISTS SAY DATURA PLANT MAY HAVE CRUSH ON RADIATION. That filler said that "researchers have noticed a greater profusion of *Datura*, also known as jimsonweed or thorn apple, near sources of nuclear radiation." Could it be true, a tropism, as we English majors learned to say, of stramonium for plutonium, uranium, and other nuclear fuels and waste, just as MacLeod said?

If it were true, could the association of a crazy-making plant, a dangerous weed, discredit nuclear power? It might be true and have no meaning, let alone those consequences. It might be one of those juxtapositions that give fleeting meaning to post-modern life something like the way they did for the ancients. The story it*self*, or both stories, might have been put together by one of Gaunt's greenlings. Or they might both be "plants," you should pardon the expression—total inventions slipped in by a media mischief maker like those in William Gibson's *Panther Moderns* or the saboteurs in Ed Abbey's *The Monkey Wrench Gang*. I've gone to newspapers and broadcasters asking to see the source of a story and been told it was off the wire or from a magazine and had been thrown out. A good anarchist could do the same. You couldn't print THATCHER ADMITS SEX CHANGE or REAGAN'S DOC SAYS HE FAKED EXAMS OF ANDROID—REAL REAGAN DIED IN 1978, but who cared about a weed and some sheep except the locals?

Somebody said that all politics is local, so maybe this was the shot heard round the world.

It was a comfort to go from the paper to Dove Cottage, where Wordsworth and other of his worthies visited and lived. I stopped to enter and wondered, as I'm sure MacLeod had, how more than two had visited. The lecture, the lady told me, was just beginning. I handed over the fee, and that also bought me her name, which was Mrs. Musgrave.

She was telling us that when Walter Scott visited he would climb out the window and walk to the inn, itself a tiny place, where he could get more drink and food than Wordsworth provided. Coleridge seemed to have had a smaller appetite, except for laudanum and Wordsworth's wife's sister, Sarah. I tried to sort it out, not really caring. Wordsworth's sister, Dorothy, was very important. She took his dictation. His wife was named Mary, his daughter Dora, and it was Mary's sister, Sarah, with whom he was smitten—though Coleridge already had a wife and daughter, both named Sarah.

Coleridge came and went, not unlike his own "person from Porlock" or "greybeard loon" of an ancient mariner. All in this tiny cottage in which people bathed twice a year and washed clothes every five weeks, whether they needed it or not. De Quincey moved here in 1809 when Wordsworth and kin moved to a larger house. De Quincey took laudanum until age seventy-three, when I assume he died. They leave out extraordinary things in these lectures; what else could have happened, a month in a treatment center? My theory was that Coleridge's and De Quincey's laudanum habits came from living with/near Wordsworth. Laudanum probably prolonged their lives. I'm surprised Scott didn't take up the stuff, too, and I wished I had a huge jug of it right that minute. Every day brought new and subtler pains from the Black Watch. Sometimes it merged into a general ache so strong that I felt dizzy and reached out for something to steady me.

When the lecture ended I asked Mrs. Musgrave if she'd seen MacLeod. "Oh my yes," she said. "He's one you don't forget. He left his card in Mr. Wordsworth's tray, something nobody's ever done before in this— what do I mean?—modern circumstance. I thought that a bit cheeky but harmless and almost charming. Then later on the back, I saw he'd written: 'I must have laudanum!' "

"Many have described him as harmless and almost charming," I told her, and she seemed reassured.

"He asked a great many questions about Wordsworth's change from a revolutionary with a French passport to a conservative. I'd guess he was experiencing something like that, though I haven't seen his work. He said he was a writer, but I confess I never heard of him. He asked me if laudanum were still available without a prescription—extraordinary, don't you think?— and I said I was sure it wasn't, though I'd never inquired. He said he'd discovered Solpadeine with codeine for purchase over the counter, as he called it. He said that the main problem in the world today was alleviating pain. He fell asleep in the poet's chair and snored through my lecture, but I didn't dare wake him. I took two more groups through before he woke. Some of them thought he was a wax dummy until they heard him snore."

* * *

Back at the Highfield, I'd just tugged off my shoes after a literary day and was thinking what a hot bath might do for my own pain when the phone rang. The owner said he had a message for me at the desk. Perhaps I'd want to come down for it rather than . . . I appreciated his discretion, I think, but it meant turning off the hot water and putting those same shoes back on and walking more.

He seemed to be enjoying the intrigue, even if I wasn't. He handed the note to me across the desk. It said simply: "Meet me at Pow and Udale Streets, Workington, noon tomorrow above the shop. Book available."

"None of my business," said Mr. Farley, "but do be careful. This fellow sounded quite furtive. I mean if you'd like someone to go along, I could. I was in the RAF and we learned some hand-to-hand. I would never presume this if you hadn't identified yourself as a detective and taken such a beating. I wouldn't mind a bit of adventure."

I thanked him almost sincerely, but said I was also a rare-book fancier and was bidding on something rather rare, which might explain the furtiveness of the voice.

"I collect the odd book myself," he said. "That can be a dangerous game, too. Anything with value, you know, crooks get a whiff. . . ." Farley sensed that his adventure would not be forthcoming and bravely went back to his newspaper. I reflected that I did have a rare magazine or two, including a Zap Comix #1.

TWENTY
◆◆◆◆

I WAS EARLY, so I drove around Workington. The last time I'd been here, it was a dirty and desperate port city, nearly deserted. Coming to it from the Lake District was like coming out of the Rockies into a trailer park in Salt Lake City. Now, to my amazement, there was fresh paint everywhere, a scaffold on every other building, a boom. There was no way to reclaim it as a seaside resort, because the harbor and port had all been claimed by the port and industry, but inland it was looking pretty good.

I drove out to the mouth of the Derwent (the river that the lake made). It was clean. The tide was ebbing and the water was remarkably clear. A few pleasure boats rode at anchor in what must be a deeper basin from which they could come ashore in dinghies. There were new waterfront pubs and inns like the Sailor's Return for merchant seamen or tourists and several rows of new houses presumably for those working portside.

I remembered from being a seaman that ports could have lovely and hidden rewards for the real sailor, but this was out in the open.

Back in town, I located the corner of Pow and Udale. That block was being renovated as well, and the shop to which my caller had referred was a Value Shoe store, empty and with CLOSING DOWN—EVERYTHING MUST GO soaped on the window. I marked the gray door that would lead above and the Chicken Shop, a poultry mart, next door, which still seemed in business, or at least in limbo. That whole corner building was obviously up for renovation, rising out of slumdom, not sinking into it. Across the street to the northeast was an upmarket men's store in a building that had already been redone. On the southeast corner was a Midlands Bank branch office. On the northeast or catercorner was the car park where I sat in my Panda. Next door on Udale to the south was a nice little neo–High Romanesque or Low Gothic church.

Raymond Chandler could have told us exactly, but I don't have his eye. I didn't grow up in a nation that had buildings older than the U.S., nor did I prep at Dulwich, nor did I experience nostalgia from displacement to southern California oil wells and the phony Tudor and other period knockoffs of Los Angeles.

My reason for studying this location was professional, I wanted to know how many doors and windows there were, whether there were one-way streets or stoplights, and what the quickest way was to the A road out of town east or the coast road north and south. Was there a regular police walking or radio-car beat? Who were in the other shops and what vantage had they on the door and upstairs?

Maybe I'd also learn something about the man who chose this location. This was right in the middle of town on a weekday, in broad daylight. I was meeting someone who was breaking the law but was also concerned for his own safety. If he was the Pict, I had already broken his arm.

My guess was that he'd bought the use of an unfurnished room or rooms up there, explaining that he needed space to sort out some papers, to store boxes, or for some other reason. Maybe he had a bunk and running water up there, but this wasn't anybody's permanent home. It was possible that he just knew how to pick the lock and planned to take his chances meeting me there and to be gone before anyone noticed.

Still an hour early, I found a chemist and gave in to my desire for pain relief. The Farleys had only aspirin. I bought Solpadeine, read the label, noted the caffeine to counter drowsiness, took two, then drove inland and found a bright, big, new pub called the Briery. It was bustling inside and a politically correct American couple was talking about how refreshing it was to introduce their young son, Jason, to real pub food. Jason, maybe seven, yanked at his mother's expensive jacket sleeve like the instantly gratified yuppie pup he was, and I wasn't sorry to see them head for the Volvo, where Jason would probably tell them that British "chips" sucked in comparison to McDonald's fries. And he'd be right.

But I didn't eat chips. I sat at the bar and ordered a pot of tea and a Ploughman's Lunch, which was bread, cheese, fruit, odd condiments and veggies, and whatever else local custom dictated. I hoped it would provide karmic balance to my codeine.

Then I asked the older gent sitting to my left the question I'd been wanting to ask somebody since I came down from the hills and lakes. "I was here in '86," I said. "Workington wasn't like this then. A boom's going on here. Can you tell me what or how or why?" It seemed the whole pub stopped talking and moving at the same time, then, having considered the question, gave the answer as one. The answer was "Sellafield."

How could I have missed it? The plant was just down the coast. "Do any of you work there?" I asked.

"I'm in procurement," said a barmaid, and laughed off the risqué jokes of her friends. "I work here for entertainment. See how funny these geezers are?"

Whatever Sellafield was doing, it had not cast a pall over its neighbors, made them lose their sense of humor, and this girl, Sylvia, was the living version of the hypothetical woman in my Green Man interrogation. She went back and forth with orders, and chipped in while the others told me how it worked. Not only had Sellafield sponsored some projects directly and lent money for others, but the payroll had expanded since they came here in the fifties (when my classmates and I were playing "duck and cover" in class nuclear attack drills and some of our parents were building bomb shelters) and that money was being spent everywhere, including here today.

I asked the same older gent if he worked at the plant. "No, I'm in public health," he said.

"Any problems there?"

"I'm only in maintenance," he said, "but we're all a bit concerned that people get leukemia more round here than elsewhere."

"Are you one of them no-nuke chaps?" Sylvia asked. "Say, I bet he's a pop star. Get his autograph." They weren't unfriendly, even if I'd said I was a no nuker.

"I'm just a traveling salesman," I said.

"And I'm the Duchess of York," Sylvia said, passing with a large tray, stopping to let me grab my Ploughman's. More laughter. Another time we might have gone somewhere after she got off both her jobs.

I ate my food, finished my tea, and thanked all for the pleasant conversation. Sylvia was near the door when I left, so I stopped and gave her what I hoped was a decent tip. "Don't work too hard," I said sincerely.

"Make hay while the sun shines," she said. I was almost through the door when she called out: " 'Bout the other? I just try not to think about it. All of us do."

TWENTY-ONE
◆◆◆◆

SOMETHING WAS WRONG at the corner of Pow and Udale. First, I noticed that the door to the stairs was open. Then I saw the Scot's van. I closed the street door and went up the stairs fast. The door to the left was open, so I went in there, wishing I had a gun.

He had a gun, my Scot. He was standing in a rubble of fallen plaster in a room that showed the lathe behind where that plaster had been. He was holding a pistol, a nice, plastic 9mm semiautomatic Glock. He was simply holding it, the barrel pointed at the rubble on the floor. His gaze was blank. Whatever had happened had happened recently. I took the pistol from him and smelled it. Not fired. There was a key in the inside hole of the door to the stairs. I walked over and turned it to lock the door and put the key into my pocket. If the Scot came alive, I didn't want him to run.

I walked through a doorway into the kitchen and saw the bathroom beyond. Other than closets, it was the only place I hadn't looked in that apartment. The Pict had been duct-taped naked to the commode, also handcuffed to a standing pipe. His right arm, which I'd broken, was in a cast. He'd been wrapped in electrical cord that had been stripped so the bare wires touched his skin, wrapped in it from his ears down to his groin. Perhaps the Scot thought that the threat of this "improvised hostile interrogation," as we'd learned to call it, would be enough. The Pict might have called his bluff, figuring I'd be along any minute to rescue him. They had both underestimated the power of this rig. I figured the Scot had plugged it in, then immediately tried to get it out as he saw what it was doing to his enemy. Too late. The Pict had evacuated his bladder and bowels, and I flushed the toilet. He wasn't even cold yet.

I saw the writing on his arms, chest, back. It was an alphabet I didn't know. I didn't think it was Hebrew or Nordic runes. I knew it wasn't Greek or Cyrillic. I didn't know, and I doubted anyone disposing of his body would, and his message would not be understood.

Yes, his body. What to do? The Pict's mouth was taped shut, so nobody had screamed. The street door was now closed. The Pict must have called from a pay phone. I walked out through the kitchen into an empty living room. I heard a rustle and saw the Scot's back in the open closet. I chambered a round, drew down on him, and made trigger contact as he turned, squeezing slowly. The Glock has a double-trigger safety. I had passed one and was squeezing the last.

He had a box. I put my finger outside the trigger guard but kept him in the sights. "It's his book," he said. "I got it back."

A man had died for Jock's book. Not a good man, but, as Robbie Burns taught them to say a little farther north, "a man's a man for a' that."

"Where'd he have it hidden?"

"In his car. I knew which one it was—the little Austin

Metro—because I had a bug in it to track him with, but I never thought he'd be that obvious. I could have taken his keys and looked, and I wouldn't have . . . I never dreamed. . . ." He was starting to tremble, and tears fell to the plaster dust, making little puffs as they hit. "I thought it would be in a bank box, a locker of some kind. He was so—"

"Stupid," I said, "but that's no excuse for killing him."

I was trying to think smart. If I called the locals on this it would throw me and the book and MacLeod's name into the slow machinery of justice, and who knew how long it might be before I could find Jock? "Do you know where MacLeod is?" I asked.

"No," he said. "I thought you'd do that and I'd get his book back, and if I couldna find him, gie it to you." He was speaking Lallans or Lowlands Scot dialect, broader under stress. "A book like this . . ." He had no words to express his hopes for this cargo cult he worshiped, this fraudulent bullshit, for all I knew, that MacLeod had turned into a crusade of some kind, a crusade for Absurdists, a riddle, a grail, a what?

I reached out and he handed it to me, and involuntarily I took it and against every instinct but one began to read. There are times when our commonest words seem exotic: *go, fork*. Just look at them there. How did they come to be? *Tooth, cork, pill, pain, fuck*. All of this first page read that way, familiar yet exotic, plain and yet indecipherable, insane or at least incoherent, yet compelling, mesmerizing. It was a little like listening to English with a wall between you and the source, or listening to a pigeon's cooing that you could swear is a human voice, and you're *that* close to understanding it.

As I stood in a web of Jock's or somebody's words, a small part of me noticed that the Scot had walked slowly away toward the kitchen and beyond. The words held me still until a larger part of me responded to a muffled cry and the sound of thrashing and the smell of burning flesh.

I ran to it and found that the Scot had first considerately taped his own mouth, then wrapped the bare wire around his arm, filled the sink with water, and, holding the sink's rim, his fingers making contact and then more of him as the water spilled over, reached out, stretching just at the feet of his victim, and pushed the plug home.

I stepped back, tossed the gun aside, scanned the kitchen, and found an old sponge, dry and stiff, but I didn't want it wet. I leaned into the bathroom and yanked the plug free, then turned off the faucet and dragged the Scot out. The smell of his burning hair was in my nostrils. I hit his thin chest, blew into his lungs, and kept on doing it until I couldn't see for my own tears and his eyes were dull and dry. I had liked him. They were both losers, not serious criminals, but this guy had a kind of innocent nobility, and I hated his death. He hadn't evacuated from the shock like the other. He'd probably been living on candy bars and gas fumes.

But I couldn't be here much longer. I wet the sponge and wiped everything I'd touched. I might have to explain this later, but there were good reasons for not trying it now. This was so strange that it would take a lot more than a third party, a pistol, and a box full of gibberish to make sense of it. One of those "You had to be there, officer," situations, and they don't like those situations.

Should I call Gaunt and see if he had a sanitation team of his own men or could still call on the Old Boys for their unquestioning assistance? I had met half the town, and, whether they got my name or not, they knew there had been a banged-up, red-eyed stranger in town, and if I left this, I would be found. When the orange-cockaded Farleys read this in the paper, they'd be on the horn pronto. If I stayed and played this straight, I'd blow the case and still risk my license everywhere but Uganda, Haiti, and Lebanon. Damn!

I had to call Gaunt. If they subjected this situation to the British tradition of ratiocination (okay, Poe invented it, but he was as loaded as De Quincey—an orangutan?), this would be a three-way struggle over a book, with me the winner and loser. I needed to be Hammett's "wild and unpredictable monkey wrench" thrown into the works, and I couldn't do that behind bars.

I went to the nearest pay phone and called him. Either they had indeed closed the secret Green Man or he was mending at home like me. He'd given me the number that would reach the lads in back, but I'd thoughtlessly left it in my baggage and anyway he was home.

"I'm already in a pay phone. Give me the number of one of yours." I wasn't sure, but I figured they might have his nearby booths covered, and if he called me, they'd connect him with Workington. This way I called him, and they might know where, but there wouldn't be time to hear us, and maybe the call from Workington along with many others wouldn't click. He didn't question but gave me a number. I walked around to a car shop and watched a man sand a fender for fifteen long minutes, then called him.

"I'll do this quick," I said.

"Yes. I should say that I got word Special Branch are interested in what seem to be unrelated strange events for which only we know the connections."

"You don't know the worst. Can you get a sanitation team?"

"We can adapt. Jesus, man, you mean wet work?"

"Yes, but not mine and not too messy, organically speaking. Accidental homicide and then suicide by the first perp. Pict and Scot. If I stay, I'll be wrapped in red tape forever."

"Not messy?"

"No. No blood. Just need a couple of workmen to take out a pair of rolled carpets or paint drop cloths. Prints not important with them gone, because no crime. No real paper trail, either. Need to remove vehicles, an Austin Metro and the Scot's van. I'll leave keys with remains. Main thing is the mortal coils themselves."

"Kept your sense of humor, I see."

"I'm giddy. It's already hitting me, though. Like that business recently. I'm looking for laudanum."

"Get me some, too. I've got a broken rib. I'm so tightly taped I can hardly breathe, and when I do it kills me. I think the thing is to get this done semiofficially, privileged alumnus status and all. Given the connections and aspirations of that last fellow, shouldn't raise any dust. And shouldn't connect to anything Special Branch are looking into. They only understand reason, anyway, the coppers. I don't care what you say about New Scotland Yard and Sherlock Holmes and all that rubbish. That lot don't understand the chaos of human behavior. Something like this, they're lost. I'll give it to MI5 subcontractors. They'll be keeping a secret from themselves, which they're good at."

"We're talking too long," I said. "I haven't even given you details."

"Take your time," Bobby said. "You sounded urgent, so I went to a *really* secure phone, which will now need to be changed. No, don't ask."

I gave him the address and circumstances so he could pass it along to the pros, the guys who cleaned up slaughterhouses and never asked why because, like many of us, they've learned to compartmentalize their lives. Some might call it denial or avoidance. Orwell might call it Doublethink. I called it lucky for now.

I already had the book and the gun, and the cuffs and keys, in my car—the book the most dangerous by far—so I headed back to Highfield, winked at Mr. Farley as I passed with the box, implying a future explanation, then called down that I'd be taking a nap until six. Emergency calls only, please.

Later, after supper, I called my employer, Mr. Ellis, to say I had the book.

"Fax it to me," he demanded.

"Are you nuts?" I asked. "Some eight hundred pages? I'm in the boondocks."

"You make England sound like the Wild West," he said, still peevish and ungrateful.

"Besides, I don't actually have it in my hands."

He started a tantrum and I hung up on him. In five minutes I called again and said, "Raise your voice, lose your detective. Pavlov's dogs could master that. Now, as I was saying, it's in a safety deposit box to which only

MacLeod has access. While I start the legal procedures just in case, I'm going to get my hands around his throat soon and drag him into . . . Manchester," I improvised, so he couldn't get involved, "and get it back. You'll get a full account in notes and narrative."

"Now don't hang up," he said, "but how tough could England be? I've been there. I mean——"

"It's not a place where Americans get quick results through official channels," I said. "But I'm lucky to have unofficial channels, which is the reason I've gotten this far. Your interests will be well served, but if you start making phone calls to lawyers and police here, you'll undo all the work I've done."

"That sounds like blackmail. You aren't working with MacLeod to scam me, are you? No, wait!"

"No, and when I get back, I'll prove it. First I'll give MacLeod such a punch that his shriveled old dick will drop off. Did I mention that in pursuit of your interest I had twenty of the meanest motherfuckers in the U.K. work me over, have lost the vision in one eye, had an ear nearly ripped from my head, had a toe broken and a finger dislocated, and that's only a partial inventory?"

"I guess there'll be a big hospital bill," he said. This jerk couldn't help it. "You know they might hold us liable if you hurt anybody over there."

"Not to worry. We in special ops care for our own wounds. But here's something you *can* hold me liable for, because when I get back with the book and MacLeod, I'm going to hit *you* so hard that everybody who ever attended your prep school will die."

He had a brief wave of common sense and remained silent for about four beats. Then he said, pouting: "I didn't go to prep school."

"Poor boy. Where'd you go to college?"

"Iowa."

"Well, then I'm going to hit you even harder, you fraudulent, cornhustling little shoat, because how could you possibly know anything about good writing? Good-bye. I'll call again when I must. If you piss me off one more time, I'll turn this novel into a homeless shelter." I hung up.

I worried about *shoat*. I thought that was a young pig. A stoat was a kind of weasel. Either way. He wouldn't look it up.

TWENTY-TWO
◆◆◆◆

I LOOKED OUT from breakfast the next morning and saw rain on the lake. A cold front was coming through and the vacationers were trying to adjust their plans. Mine were to head north, up past the walls the Romans built, to the land of the Scots. As I crossed the border on the way to Ayr, I had a strange sense of familiarity. Then I realized it was because it looked like Appalachia. Just as the Lake District had suggested the best of New England and the south coast my own Pacific Northwest, this part of Scotland could have been North Carolina or Tennessee. I saw my first billboards, litter, mill outlet shops, and a sign at a gas station inviting citizens to play for "Dynasty Dollars," meaning the American TV show "Dynasty."

Ayr had every chance to be a beautiful seacoast town, but it suffered from the same backwardness. MacLeod's mood couldn't have been improved by the Elms Court Hotel, an establishment mainly for commercial travelers for the more desperate products. I negotiated a quiet "special room" behind the main building and off the road, where there'd be nobody to smoke in the halls and elevators or keep me awake hawking up the day's accumulated nicotine sputum.

If I'm hard on the Scots, it's because, as I said earlier, I'm 100 percent one kind of Celt or another, and I'm sick of apologizing for us. MacLeod had written a screed in the guest book:

> As Mr. Dunbar, your good sixteenth-century poet and patriot wrote of his fellows, how can this Stone Age habit persist of simply throwing garbage out of the dwelling, which is only one step beyond throwing it into the corner? So far, the great advance Dunbar noted with irony is that his fellow citizens of Edinburgh agreed more or less on a time to do it, around nine at night, as if it would not be there if not seen in winter darkness, or as if some magic would remove it before dawn.
>
> I can only believe that those additional centuries of civilization the Romans gave the south have not been compensated for here, or that it's the pain of feeling unfairly treated as Scots or Welsh or Irish that makes us strike back like monkeys, by hurling offal. I say good-bye with an almost physical heartache. This, my first Scottish city, built on a lovely coast, is haunted day and night by great, flapping ghosts of litter—newspapers, food containers, plastic bags, perhaps shreds of Celtic honor. Sadly, James MacLeod

I thanked the concierge for showing it to me and for his special room, and I followed the thanks with a big tip. He was a quiet and agreeable man with a wispy mustache and mousy hair, in contrast to the strong, clefted chin of a matinee idol. "Something to what he says," he said. "Suppose he'd mind if I sent it in to the paper?"

"No, he'd expect it. Please do. By the way, I've seen great progress since I was here in '86."

My only disappointment in my special arrangement at the Elms Court was the kipper breakfast, and I ordered it myself. I made a copy of the book, put it into a safety deposit box, and mailed the key with instructions to the sisters.

I drove inland to Ecclefechan, Carlyle's birthplace, named for Fechan, an early missionary to the pagan Celts. I only checked the book at the Burns house and, as I suspected, Jock had not been there. He wasn't a big fan of Burns, not with Carlyle so close. Ecclefechan was a small crossroads on mainly open moor—just a few houses, one of them Thomas Carlyle's, and a concrete plant close behind it, only a few feet behind the tiny cemetery where Carlyle lay, spending an eternity yelling "Quiet!" And to think he'd declined burial in Westminster Abbey for this.

I stood looking around at the arch to an inner courtyard his mason father had built and the locked door of what the sign said was the Carlyle Museum and birthplace until a woman came from across the road to let me in. From here Carlyle had walked for three days to the university at Edinburgh at age thirteen to study mathematics, and when he had quickly mastered that, he went on to learn everything else. It was still possible then for prodigies like him and his opponent in the slavery debate, John Stuart Mill, to command all of human knowledge, from geography to Greek.

It was strange to hear the grind of concrete trucks and

the rip of fighter planes, ours and the Brits, across the barren moors. Our Emerson had sought out Carlyle here, the lady told me, and all the great men and women of his generation knew him, if only by reputation, which was fully as thorny—nay, worse—than Mac-Leod's. Jock had charm.

Mrs. Thompson remembered MacLeod, all right. "We don't get that many visitors. Your Mr. MacLeod [Why did they all call him *my* Mr. MacLeod?] said it was because only great and difficult souls like Carlyle would seek him out, then and now. Oh, he wrote a lot in the book, and while he considered what to write, he wore the man's big, black hat and carried his walking stick. I dinna ken how to say nay to it. It was much like havin' the master here again, though of course I dinna know him.

"MacLeod went back and gave the men at the concrete plant such a blessing out I thought they'd come to blows. Turned out they decided to take a holiday. It was either that, the boss told me later, or give him a thrashing. Here's what he wrote."

She handed me the book, with a few entries—the first visitor to this shrine after Carlyle's death was a man from Massachusetts in March of 1883—and then MacLeod's outburst, but first I looked up to see a framed photograph on the wall. I couldn't help laughing.

"He had the same reaction," said Mrs. Thompson. "It seems the mother bears a strong resemblance to an American comedian named Woody Allen. I've not seen Mr. Allen, so I canna say." She paused, hesitated, then spoke in a different tone. "Oh, you must be his friend, Mr. Sierra, as he said would follow along. He's written in there for you. You're the next guest after him. I dinna know how I could have forgotten that.''

She moved to a discreet distance while I read, skimming, trying to be a detective and not increasingly his Boswell. But damn if he didn't try to nail it right to me.

Sierra, you'll be my Boswell. As you know by now, I'm a *sennaiche*, a carrier and teller of stories in the oral Celtic tradition. I can almost see you shaking your head, though I haven't seen your head in so long. We'll meet soon, I hope. I'm still heading north, up along the moors where anything can still happen. They've brought a sonar boat to Loch Ness to look for Nessie. The last ''scientific'' search was two men in a rowboat with a lead weight and line. Hah!

You may sense that I'm feeling some disappointment in my forebears. The price of dreaming. I learn now that my progenitor's name, *Liotr*, may not mean fierce wolf at all, but ''ugly.'' Go to Culloden, for I'll leave more clues there, but I'm already somewhat disarmed [Hah!] by reading last night that while a Hugh MacLeod fought for Bonnie Prince Charlie against that fat-assed German Cumberland and the redcoats, most MacLeods were on the British side.

This seems to have happened because their chief, a Norman MacLeod, had tried in 1739 to sell most of his clansmen into indentured servitude. Telling them they were on some short errand, he shipped them out. When the ship put in at Ireland for water, they heard rumors of his betrayal and came back. Since he'd already spent the money, the Brits were steamed, but instead of skinning him, his betrayed kinsmen fought for the British to keep him from jail. At Culloden! What is clan and kin but institutionalized brutality and ignorance? This is the same as our own Civil War, and the South, like the Scots, while the more romantic and fierce, were fighting for the wrong principles.

Carlyle was rabidly pro slavery and mocked Africans in unforgivable ways, though I wonder if he'd ever seen one. Not that there was any honor fighting for the Hanoverians, a lot of belching Germans with Irish mercenaries like the Wild Geese, the Black Watch Scots, MacLeods, and others.

I'll drink no more Scotch. Bourbon's the thing for claritas and gravitas, and veritas to boot. See you on the battlefield, soldier.

—Jocko

I drove north the next day toward Culloden. The moors looked more and more like the Dakota badlands where the Sioux, like the Scots, had won and lost their great battles. I remembered Dr. Johnson's description of the moors as "so depressing as to make a man wish to hang himself, if only he could find a tree." I liked it.

The battlefield was very well preserved and managed. I watched a tape, the main point of which was the brilliant British strategy. Cumberland released copies of forged Scots orders to give no quarter, take no prisoners. This created a hatred in his own troops that took days to run its course and shamed the British army. Second, he told his infantry that when they met the famed and ferocious Celtic charge, they should bayonet the man on their right all along the line. The Scots were looking at the man before them, but their death came by indirection.

I expected a major screed here and was somewhat disappointed to read:

> I, James MacLeod, writer and *sennaiche*, do disavow any connection with others of that name. Further, from this day forward I will drink only Bourbon whiskey or the occasional glass of vodka. The point is: No more Scotch! What I need is my own Flora Macdonald. Sierra, I tell you to watch every word of a great writer. Now use your Spanish cabeza and take to ARMS!

MacLeod's handwriting was bold and beautiful. He was probably very close to a blackout or may have been in one, but the clue wasn't tough. Lewiston ARMS in Drumnadrochit. God, he must be smashed, driving this vast, gray-blue-violet terrain as we tilt with the earth toward the midnight sun of full summer.

I didn't go there but chose to spend the night in my car and walk the battlefield alone the next morning. I had my own ghosts of Culloden, and war.

Then I did begin driving north, on and on, only my compass—never drive without one—reassuring me of my northing, until I came upon the shore of Loch Ness, largest body of fresh water in the British Isles. I got out and stretched and looked at the legend, or one legend. The other, MacLeod, what was he to this? His performance had built so quickly that this last act had to be pretty damn good. Would he find and slay the monster, or tame it with Bourbon? Was he like some great, pelagic billfish, hooked and dancing on the surface one last time before sounding, or was I confusing the image with Hemingway's old man? See, MacLeod was *all* image, so a tangle of metaphors was inevitable at the climax to which he'd led me. If my obsession now matched Ahab's, did his have the power of Moby Dick? Or maybe he was just the old salmon who'd returned here to spawn legends and die.

They'd forced the highlanders out after Culloden: "The Clearances." What instinct had driven Jock here? Did he hope to repopulate these vast, blue, haunted moors with his own spirit? Vanity. Up here he was only one of hundreds of thousands of brave ghosts.

I stood and waited for the sun to set, but it didn't seem likely any time soon, and I was hungry, and I saw a sign that said Drumnadrochit was only twelve miles, so I took the lake shore drive east. The Lewiston Arms was a modern building and had a nice, quiet room for me in the back, upstairs overlooking the courtyard. I sat in the dining room with three tables of other diners, ordered my soda water and salmon, which claimed to be fresh and Scottish, and was anticipating my salad when Brother Michael, the Benedictine ball hog, God's point guard, the consummate con man of Downside Abbey, asked if he could join me. "We have a lot to talk about," he said.

"Too much monk-y business," I said, "but we can

try. Your patient and client has the Big Bowwow, as Carlyle called it, but can he bite?"

"It's important that you understand that he is a patient. He's ill. He's been with us this whole time."

TWENTY-THREE
◆◆◆◆

THE NEXT MORNING we drove south. Michael said good-bye to his fellow monk, who had driven him up here so we could talk on the way home. I'd been unwilling to listen the previous evening, calling him Benedictine Arnold and pouting and going to bed early, which I badly needed anyway. I'd make him hold his story as punishment, and I refused even to tell him I had the book.

"I know you're angry," he said, "but remember your own recovery. Once I had Jock three days off the sauce, I began to see some hope. He was in the guest house, guarded, I should add, when you came through. He very nearly broke away from us, he was so excited that you were nearby. He said, 'Didn't I tell you he was something?' "

"You're just trying to butter me up," I said.

"You know as well as I do," he said, "that every sober day is a great advance, worth more as a cure than any theory or therapy. Time's the healer. We needed time."

"You sent me on a wild-goose chase. Literally."

"No, there were those unsavory characters. You might have had to deal with them. You were paid to do that and get the book back. They might have come back to hurt Jock."

"Why, if they had the book?"

"I don't know. Weren't they at cross-purposes? That's your job. We had the forlorn hope that the book might be recovered, but that's not the most important thing. Jock's sobriety is."

"I got the damn book, and those characters won't cause any more trouble."

"Yes, praise God," Michael said, slapping me on three different sore spots three different times. I stopped the car.

"You drive. I'm very sore. I got the shit beat out of me."

"Tell, tell," Michael begged, like a kid.

"Client confidentiality. Also secret vows to a brotherhood of my own."

Michael frowned as if to say I was just being spiteful.

"I'm not kidding," I said. "It's *very* serious and I absolutely can*not* tell anyone, not *even* my client."

"I'm sorry," he said. "I hope you can eventually forgive me. I did what I thought was best."

We drove along. I began to relax. He cleared his throat. "May I see it?" he asked.

"Pull over."

I got it from the trunk and switched with him again so he could read, rifling the pages, making little noises and literally quivering with excitement. I'd spent an hour or so with it last night and knew a little of what he was feeling.

After nearly an hour, he said, "Does it look, sound familiar to you?"

"Reminds me a bit of *Finnegans Wake*, but I never

read more than a few pages of that. I did read *Ulysses*. My guess as I copied it page by page in Ayr was that he substituted Edinburgh for *Wake*'s Dublin, but then I thought, there's little of Scotland in this, or Ireland. Whatever this is, it has that flavor, but it's *sui generis*, some land of bars and their denizens that the writer imagined. It was word-drunk, words with power but no meaning. It was like reading a work of mad genius in another language, although it was English, or Irelish, or Scotlish."

"Very few readers have finished *Finnegans Wake*," Michael said, "but I have, and this is not it."

"Imagine," I said, "if you took the meaning from words and kept their beauty—say the way painters abstract color, form, and so on. Then imagine boundless energy to keep on doing that, a kind of aesthetic that would guide the writer and a boundless confidence and compulsion to do wordplay on such a grand scale. What would be required? Use Occam's razor? What's the simplest answer that fits these vastly complex circumstances, that will, Brother Michael, explain the phenomenon in your lap?"

He took his time as I drove south, popping two more Solpadeines and escaping his notice altogether as he used his training. He was no Jesuit, but he was no dummy. Finally he said, "Schizophrenia."

"Elementary, my dear Watson," I said, enjoying this first experience of solving a case with logic of a sort. "And is Jock MacLeod schizophrenic?"

"No," he said without pause. "He's a drunk, not psychotic. Not that great writers like Joyce don't sometimes approach the joy of sheer wordplay of the schizoid personality at times. One can tell."

I had more for my Watson. "Then whom do we know who is schizophrenic, capable of such a book, which I consider nonetheless a work of genius?"

He shook his head. Of course he didn't know. He hadn't shared our youth, shouted and oinked and "blagged" in and outside the Wild Boar. He hadn't known Non-Linear Lenny, nor been worshiped by him, nor been the recipient of Lenny's magnum opus upon his death: a box that no doubt arrived in the mail after a phone call from a lawyer, not long ago; a box whose contents still haunted some stunned typist somewhere—Jock being too lazy even to type it; a box that had earned a million dollars and had been stolen and for which two men had already died.

"The author is a man we knew years ago. We called him Non-Linear Lenny. I remember how he would recite this some nights in the bar. My guess is he's dead and left the novel to Jock, and you know everything from there, Watson."

"So if Jock wanted you on this case, he at least subconsciously wanted you to find him out?"

"Possible. But I'm still going to kick his butt."

"It strikes me as important to publish," Michael said.

"But not under Jock's name," I said.

"He needs a book."

"I don't give a red rat's ass what he needs. This may belong to him as property, but not as his creation."

Michael paused. "Yet he was instrumental in its writing, contributed his guidance and . . . spirit to the project. In a way, it's about him."

"Perhaps we should call in the Jesuits," I said. "Don't they know more about copyright law, angels on pinheads, subtle distinctions?"

"But not as much about show-business contracts in general," he said, chuckling.

"If you think you're going to jolly Friar Tuck me into letting MacLeod's name go onto this book, think again."

"But MacLeod needs a book, and the publisher didn't buy a book by your non-linear, tragic friend."

"Let MacLeod fucking-A write one."

He paused. "How about something like 'co-spontaneous authorship' for both?"

"How about immaculate conception? No deal." I paused. "I can live with 'presented by its inspiration, Jock MacLeod.' "

"Hmmmm," Brother Michael hummed. "With an introduction by me, a not unworthy scholar who feels that this may be the literary event of the decade, perhaps even bordering on the miraculous. How did the Bible come to us, after all?"

"I'm afraid it was through guys like you," I said. "You and Saint Paul. Barnum and Bailey. Is there anything you won't do?"

"I won't lie. This is . . . presentation, but it has to be essentially true."

"And Lenny's heirs must be contacted, if there are any, and they get a big share."

"And the abbey a small share—a modest share. I do seriously intend to get MacLeod sober or die trying."

"Don't ask me to choose," I joked. "That's a tough call." We laughed. "You're leaving out this weasel editor. I know him. He won't go for this freak show."

Michael thought some more as we began to see the occasional tree. "He will if we also offer the best-ever private-eye novel, your own record of the search for

MacLeod and the mystery of the book. Can't make Jock look like a thief, of course."

"Not on your probably-doomed-to-roast-in-hell life, padre. I haven't even decided if I'll let Jock live. I can't tell you, but I could face serious consequences if I tell this story."

"Leave it to me," he said, like a tonsured Swifty Lazar. "It's all in how you present the message. Even without the dodgy stuff, it's a winner. You know I'd give ten quid to hear Stevie Wonder sing 'Superstition' right now." I turned on the radio—BBC-2, I think— and, since it was that kind of day, there he was. I held out my hand and Michael slapped it, and we bounced along seat-dancing and singing until the news came on.

"Today's top story is the massive migration toward Stonehenge for summer solstice from all over Britain. The police had vowed to control the regular attempts to visit the monument by so-called hippies and other road migrants, but the appearance of American writer/guru Jock MacLeod and his announcement of a message seems to have overthrown all previous plans."

"Shit," I said.

To his credit, Michael said, "Jesus help us."

As we drove south at much higher speeds, the sky darkened and it began the kind of steady rain that you know must be widespread. The police were no longer trying to keep anyone out, but negotiations were on-going between them and "spokespersons" who didn't seem to know anything. MacLeod was said to be coming in the afternoon for a speech and an all-night be-in to wait for the sun to rise and shine through the monument with the amazing accuracy that has for centuries amazed us. Meanwhile, a sound system had been per-

mitted and bands were trying to play, partly in competition with individual ravers' enormous noise boxes.

The mud was universal—worse than Woodstock, according to veterans of that event—and nobody knew
quite what to do with a situation that seemed out of
control from the beginning.

"Is he just making this his big publicity move?" I
wondered. All our information was coming from the
radio.

Brother Michael tried optimism. "If he's broken out
to make that announcement—unless, come to think of
it, he could have made it from the abbey. . . . Maybe we
should pray for him not to be drunk."

"And pray for all those who'll be trampled to death
in the mud," I added. "You know if he made that
announcement he's loose and drinking again."

"Could someone have made it without his permission?" Michael wondered desperately.

I thought of Bobby Gaunt. "Anything's possible.
Maybe the police want an excuse to break this hippie
cycle once and for all, but I don't think so. I think our
boy's having one last crow."

The radio finally mentioned that television and film
cameras had been allowed access to the event.

"He's out," I said glumly, "and Stonehenge's got
him."

T W E N T Y - F O U R
◆◆◆◆

By THE TIME we got to Stonehenge we were half a million strong, according to the radio, and the Arch Druid MacLeod had been seen. We got as far as we could, then locked the Panda and joined the other pilgrims in the mud. People everywhere were shedding their clothes, just throwing them away. Some had painted their faces, but most of it washed off in the rain. I borrowed some white unwashable and put a cross on the roof of the Panda, a trick Travis McGee had taught me.

It was clear that a great quantity of drugs had already been consumed. People danced by themselves to un-heard music and passed "roll-ups" that were too wet to smoke. Drinking seemed the easiest high, and by far the most popular in this early going. There were empties of all kinds everywhere under foot.

There was a stirring to our right and I saw something I didn't expect: a group of men in berets. They were wearing neither the paratrooper red nor the SAS sand-colored berets but forest green ones with sprigs of what looked like mistletoe. As they came closer, I realized they were wearing jumpsuits, black balaclavas under their berets, and H&K MP-5s, with a few shotguns. They also carried police riot shields made of Kevlar. I realized that the Glock was still in my trunk. Just as well. I yelled at them and used a tactical arm gesture we'd all used in basic, and they waved us over. I recognized Bobby Gaunt's large, strong hand as he reached out to touch my shoulder, and in the midst of the Roman tortoise shield formation, in Druid white, now mud-splattered, with a sporran over his waist, with a MacLeod tartan tam with a sprig of mistletoe atop, and with a long ceremonial stick topped with some ceremonial knob, was the High Blaggar himself, Jocko MacLeod.

"Gat, come, let me hug you," he said, his eyes leaking rain and tears, his balance needing assistance from his bodyguards. Emma was with him, like Mary Magdalen with Christ, and wouldn't meet my gaze.

"Don't think you're getting out of this alive," I told Jock. "You've got a lot to answer for, you great, bloated, sagging bag of *haggis*. Not all the SAS men in the world can keep me from you."

Gaunt waved them off. I figured they were guys from the Green Man taking a big chance, which was why the chopper stood nearby. It wore the markings of CNN, probably a forgery. Gaunt had a big role in this, and I was, once more, left out.

"I forgive you," Jock said. "God forgives us all." They led him to the podium made of piled-up crates and to the lectern and microphone. Oh, God, I thought. This might actually be a historic moment and I might not be able to kill him. But we had good seats. I rubbed mud onto my face, pointing to the cameras, and Michael did the same.

"We didn't all come here with pure hearts and motives," he said, his voice quieting the multitudes, "but we must all leave that way. An extraordinary thing will happen not far from here tomorrow with the dawn of summer's longest day. I may not be here. I won't be there because I know only its timing, not its nature." How could he speak so clearly and be so drunk?

"These," he said, holding up his right hand and rummaging through the sporran he'd worn over his robe, "are seeds of awakening. They are from the datura plant, called also thorn apple and jimsonweed. They are poisonous in most forms, hallucinogenic in carefully—"

He was interrupted by a roar from the crowd, which looked for all the world like the end of the world in a film by Terry Gilliam. Without the choppers and lights and cameras and mikes, it could have been the Dark Ages, and maybe it was just that.

MacLeod tried to play down the crowd's appetite for hallucinogens, and continued: "These plants represent ancient knowledge, and they have a strange attraction to our most modern poison, nuclear radiation. Where these plants thrive, radiation levels must be suspect. Perhaps I should not say they're attracted by radiation, but that they wish to consume it, as ancient secrets must be recovered to consume our modern technological sins."

How did he stand up, let alone command such eloquence? Clearly Emma was enthralled. Or was she looking loyally and steadily at him so as not to catch my eye and the question, How could you? Groupie! If she was moth to flame, I thought, then the sooner burned the better. I'm a poor loser.

"This is dangerous business," said our magus, to which I could not resist yelling from my muddy vantage: "No shit?"

He went on. "These plants have come to us for the purpose of pointing to danger. To those who say to you that they're dangerous and kill and make people crazy, say: What of nuclear radiation, the needless and unnatural and deadly technology to which poison they're drawn?"

The crowd roared, understanding little of it. This was not the Oxford Union.

"Mark where they grow," Jock advised. "Learn their lessons deeply. Do *not*, I repeat do not ingest or use these in any way as a drug, but take them"—here he flung the seeds abroad in a dramatic gesture, though they were stuck together by his damp grip and seemed to land pretty much in a lump in one place—"to all the corners of the human realm and plant them as a counterforce, a natural enemy, the first predator of nuclear deviltry!"

The drama of his peroration was undercut by the mad scramble of the crowd to seize and eat the seeds. It was insane. Even MacLeod recoiled in horror. He couldn't have anticipated this, in his smug self-worship. They were rooting like hogs, fighting like dogs for datura seeds.

But to my surprise and his credit, he had anticipated them. "Shame on you," he bellowed. "Like swine with pearls, Gadarene swine o'er a cliff you were warned of. I told you those seeds were death, and you're eating them."

"I didn't get none," a raver complained.

"Well," said MacLeod, "they're *not* datura. They're

only squash seeds, and I hope they grow out of your dirty ears. You are not worthy of the secrets I brought you, or of this place.

"Listen to me!" he screamed in a hoarse voice, weaving, his pulpit sinking into the mud. "Grow up, you irresponsible, drug-soaked, self-indulgent brats. Stop primping ugly before your broken mirrors, cut your hair, turn off that shitty music you listen to. Have you ever heard the Grateful Dead? Now *that's* music! How grateful we should be if you were dead, you muddy parasites. Go home. Take a bath. Get a fucking job!"

He was raving, a raver, and the crowd was getting ugly. Bobby shot off a flare and the fake CNN chopper rose and came toward us. The SAS pretenders gave the crowd a burst in the mud to move them back from trying to climb onto the unstable crate stage.

"We're booking," Bobby shouted to me, and reached his big hands down for me and the monk. "Here," he said, giving me his Beretta.

The chopper flew overhead and dropped a cargo net. We all got into it somehow, Bobby's boys clubbing off hippies who for some reason wanted to follow us skyward, and the winch cranked us up smartly, considering the weight involved, while the chopper rose away from the stage. We scrambled aboard and somebody got the door shut.

"Bobby," I yelled. "The book's in the car."

"I said we're booking," he said, misunderstanding, thinking I didn't know that book meant split, bug out.

"The novel. It's important," I said. I didn't want to drive back to Ayr. "Let me go down the rope and I'll just get it from the car and hang as we book."

"Can you find it?" he asked.

"Black roof, white cross on it." Thanks, McGee.

"There," Bobby said, pointing out the Panda. He threw me a pair of asbestos-lined gloves. He gave me the bitter end of the rope while he secured the other. I'd learned years ago from an old boatswain's mate to make a flying bowline, a quick way to make a loop if your boat's drifting past a mooring. I made one. Thanks, Boats.

I threw out the looped end, put my hiking boots on either side of the rope, grabbed it with the gloves, and went down smoking, the rain having lubed the rope just about right. I'd checked to be sure I had my keys. I threw off the gloves, opened the boot, stuffed the Glock under my waistband, held the novel box close against my chest with my right hand, slammed the boot shut, held the rope with my left, thrust my left boot into the loop, and nodded for the pilot to go.

We rose above the crowds, and I had the best seat in the house for the vast muckup that was Stonehenge Woodstock. I hung there until we were clear and the pilot set her down in a meadow, scattering sheep. I stepped aside for him to land, then climbed aboard, and they pulled in the rope.

I handed Brother Michael the box. MacLeod was looking whipped in the rear, with Emma watching.

"There's two vans," Bobby yelled. "We'll switch and ditch. This lad's got to get the chopper under cover fast."

Soon we came into a farmyard where two vans were parked. Two of Bobby's men peeled off the CNN logos. The pilot went up and away like a pheasant flushed from the brush. Bobby threw me the keys for one gray van. He and his boys got into the other. "Watch the telly tomorrow," he said. "I reckon we've subverted the dominant paradigm a bit, haven't we?"

I nodded and smiled and they left ahead of us, turning north as we turned south, toward Downside. Because it was almost the year's longest day, there was still daylight when we got to Downside. Michael helped Jock out. Emma gave me one look and said, "He needs me."

I said, "Michael, where's a shower so I can wash the pig and other shit off me, and a bed to myself? You can mind the Druid and his handmaiden later. You take care of your soldiers first."

Michael was coming my way, thinking to satisfy me and get to Jock later, when Jock turned and threw off his robe. He stood in only his tam and twig, and tattoos all over his body of ancient dragons, cups, lances, and green men. He looked like an ancient Pict, but his tattoos probably came from Liverpool. They were so fresh that they hadn't stopped bleeding, and they'd made a lovely, delicate veronica of bloody patterns from his stigmata on the inside and more subtly on the outside of his robe.

"Don't wash that," I said. "A thousand years from now it could be a relic."

"It's clear you and I must fight," Jock said, rhetorical because he didn't expect it to happen. "I'll fight you like a true Celt, naked."

It was a terrible sight, and it took a certain moxie to do what he'd done, but I was too tired to be conned. He was claiming honor while stealing virtue. Like Ronald Reagan. I was sick of him.

"And I'll fight you like a true sailor," I said. I walked over and put an overhand right smack on his upper lip, smashing it and knocking out his two upper incisors. "Or as the hippies say, 'You got pissed and got lairy, so I twatted you.' How's reality feel?" I shook my hand because it had cut me a bit. He was spitting out his teeth, holding them in amazement. I didn't help him up. That was Emma's job, his Flora Macdonald. "I should have done that twenty years ago, Jocko."

I couldn't believe it, but he got onto his feet and walked over to me again. "In my youth," he tried to say, but with his teeth out it came out "in my use."

"Not in your youth or in your use could you ever take me," I said. "Never again. Go to bed." He walked away, dignity even in his shriveled and tattooed buttocks. He had something. Maybe Emma needed it.

TWENTY-FIVE
◆◆◆◆

THE NEXT DAY it was all over the telly about the near disaster at Sellafield. Although the management denied any problem, people far into the Lake District could hear the warning claxon that signals an evacuation. Most had fled inland in panic, though nobody was hurt. The claxon stopped after some ten minutes, and the only evidence of anything untoward—though the Sellafield management had not admitted the police, who didn't really want to go anyway but were seeking a court order for a team to investigate in full radiation gear—was an oak tree on the grounds that had been incinerated by some incredible heat. There had also been a mysterious overnight shower of seeds and fruit that resembled horse chestnuts.

We were hardly on speaking terms, and only Michael asked me what I thought it was. He'd sent some brothers to retrieve my Panda. I didn't say because I was sworn, but I had it figured. A light private plane scattered the datura seeds and fruit, and they *would* grow. The claxon, I'd guess, was enormous, powered by one or two twelve-volt car batteries. It had been floated over Sellafield security fences by a large helium balloon, perhaps radio-guided as far as a likely tree, then allowed to be tangled in its branches. The claxon would go off by remote control and be timed for ten minutes. Toward the end, a higher level noise might be arranged, in case security people had found it and were close—to frighten them back for their protection. At that point a cluster of thermite grenades would be detonated, generating such heat as to destroy all evidence as well as the tree and surrounding grass. Skilled investigators might read the signs of thermite, but the people would remember only the burning bush and the claxon that the trusted nuclear stewards denied. A real Hayduke job.

I had my own work to do. Writing was hard, as Jock knew from his distant past and as I was learning now. My mood hadn't improved. I'd called Canterbury Bob and been told that he was "gone." I asked if he'd be back and the woman said she was afraid not. Was I Mr. Sierra? Yes. Bob left a message: "He said he's gone to pay his respects to Raymond Chandler. He said to remember, Bob's your uncle."

"You're being cruel to him," Emma said, but she didn't stay and defend him in the bathroom where Jock sweated, whined, and farted. Some amanuensis. Connie was on the way and would put her in the deep shade. That was not what Jock had planned at all. "This is a new world," he tried to convince me. "All things are possible with love. I'm sober."

"Only because you're handcuffed to the can," I said. "Save it for the mudpuppies. We've got a book to write, and a deadline." I was at a desk outside his bathroom and he was sitting on the throne, sweating bourbon and grandiosity. There was a canteen in the sink, so I reckoned all his needs were met.

The deal with Ellis was to get this on tape and he'd get somebody to type it, and Jock and I would share credit and payment, the last time we'd share anything. I absently picked up the Glock, which had a round in the chamber should anything disturb the Muse. I squinted down the slide through the sights then laid it down and readied the microrecorder.

"You understand, Jock, that your job is to add detail to flesh out my account, which is rather spare. You'll have to imagine the feelings of the various characters who are affected by your antics. Some of this is in a kind of narrative, but I'm not a writer, not like you."

He moaned. "I'm blocked." I'd had the Glock threaded for a suppressor so I wouldn't disturb the monastic or school programs. I put a round just above his head, into the bathroom drywall. Jock seemed less blocked.

"How's this for starters?

"In World War I German soldiers were instructed to aim first at the bagpiper who accompanied British troops—a strike against morale. . . . So when I heard Jock MacLeod's name after all those years, I figured somebody'd finally bagged the noisy, wheezy old bastard."